MOTOR CITY

MOTOR CITY

*The Odyssey of the War on Drugs, Scales of Injustice
and Two of America's Most Wanted*

SHERRI JEFFERSON

Library of Congress Cataloging-in-Publication Data is available
ISBN 10-digit 0965465659
13-digit 978-0-96546565-6

"After us, there will be no other."
D

TABLE OF CONTENTS

PART SIX: 2009 – PRESENT, AMERICA'S SHAME. 89

AUTHOR'S NOTE

Some of the names, characters, places, and incidents are used fictitiously. An organization, person, place or thing referred to in this work as a source, information, or citation is not an endorsement. This book relies on scholarly research to address anti-drug legislation and the role of four presidential administrations.

I do not endorse drug trafficking as a trade. I do oppose disparity and arbitrary and discriminatory enforcement of laws or unconstitutional laws that are vague or void for vagueness. I do not accept the dichotomy between public safety, the impact of drugs in America, and knowingly violating the Constitutional safeguards accorded Americans.

This avenue of information should be considered and applied to cure the miscarriage of justice. Alternatively, this work can be used to amend or vacate sentences, subject sentences to be commuted or pardon against persons' subject to sentencing under the Continuing Criminal Enterprise statute, mandatory minimums, "3-Strikes", and sufferers of disparate impact.

Imagine a person who is released from prison standing in front of two doors, one reads "Re-Entry" and the other "Revolving." Those doors represent the shame associated with the American criminal justice system.

"Justice is on the witness list, waiting to be called by the Court to testify truthfully."
Sherri Jefferson

INTRODUCTION

**"As my sufferings mounted, I soon realized that there were
two ways in which I could respond to my situation: either
to react with bitterness, or seek to transform the suffering
into a creative force. I decided to follow the latter course."
Martin Luther King, Jr.**

Seventy million Americans now have a criminal record. The
United States spends $80 billon dollars per year on
incarceration, almost twice the amount for education. This
book is an examination of how the issues of drugs, race, and
class became intertwined in the lives of the Motor City
Brothers as they became two of America's Most Wanted. This
material contributes to the ongoing problems of the so-called
War on Drugs by highlighting anti-drug policies, social
reform, and the criminal defense of the Motor City Brothers.
This is not a definitive history of every event concerning the
war on drugs or the Motor City Brothers. This exposition of
the counterproductive results of said war include the
execrable treatment of Blacks, Latinos, and the poor in
America.

The odyssey of the Motor City Brothers is not a tale
glamorizing drugs, material possessions, or money; it is about
how brothers David (aka D-Money) and Solomon (aka Cali)

Johnson, from inner city America – the Motor City – rise to fame and fortune by allegedly building a business that involved international drug trafficking. Follow the journey of the Motor City Brothers, from Michigan to the United States penitentiary. Purportedly, for almost two decades the Johnson brothers were the subject of an investigation led by the most elite law enforcement and intelligence agencies in the world: the DEA, FBI, and CIA, as well as a High Intensity Drug Trafficking Area (HIDTA) task force; the latter was authorized by the HIDTA program, enacted as part of the Anti-Drug Abuse Act of 1988, and enables law enforcement to obtain assistance from task forces in areas determined to be critical drug-trafficking regions of the United States.

In 2005, the brothers were captured after an ongoing investigation and subject to eight indictments, which included 41 different named defendants, many who used aliases; however, upon careful review and consideration of their entire case record, it is clear that both brothers were the victims of ineffective assistance of counsel and denial of a speedy trial. The basic rights afforded to any person accused of a crime in the United States were violated. Victims of such ineffective assistance, the brothers were sentenced by a United States District Court judge to a pine box sentence of 30 years, with a $270 million-dollar judgment. A pine box sentence is a prison term that almost guarantees death beyond the wall; the convicted person leaves prison in a coffin.

At the time of their sentencing, David (aka D-Money) Johnson was 40 and Solomon (aka Cali) Johnson was 38; the government alleged that their plea was an acceptance of culpability for being the leaders of the D-Money Johnson (DMJ) criminal enterprise. The pine box sentence includes 20 years for money laundering as the underlying felony offense under the Continuing Criminal Enterprise statute. The Johnson brothers did not plea to drug trafficking, possession of drugs, or violent offenses.

PROLOGUE

"So that we do not relive our past, we must relearn it."
Sherri Jefferson

America's shame. The declaration of the so-called War on Drugs began in 1971, a few years after the death of Dr. Martin Luther King, Jr., and the signing of the Civil Rights Act of 1964 and the Voting Rights Act of 1965. The war is so-called because our nation has not engaged in a war on drugs, but rather launched an assault on addicts and regulated the activities of certain groups of people. The people most affected by it are people suffering from mental health and escaping their realities of poverty, loss of employment, and educational opportunities. The war has hurt drug addicts, families of people in prison, and others whose lives have been destroyed by violence associated with drugs.

If the war on drugs is the equivalent to an actual war, then it is the longest war ever fought by the United States of America. For the last 44 years, the U.S. has engaged in warfare that has resulted in more causalities and fatalities than any other war in its history. From 1980 to 2008, the number of people incarcerated in America quadrupled - from roughly 500,000 to 2.3 million people – and with only 5% of the world population, the U.S. now has 25% of all the world's prisoners. The U.S. correctional population - those in jail, prison, on probation or on parole - now totals 7.3 million, or 1 in every 31 adults. America's shame.

African Americans have more men and women incarcerated in state prisons than any other race or ethnic group. They represent 37% of the total federal prison population, but only 12% of the total U.S. population. According to the Sentencing Project, "There are 283,000 Hispanics in federal and state prisons and local jails, making up slightly over 15% of the inmate population. Nearly 1 in 3 (32%) persons held in federal prisons is Hispanic." America's shame.

The majority of these prisoners are incarcerated on non-violent drug related offenses. As subjects of the penal system, they suffer the collateral consequences associated with arrest and conviction, which include problems with their H.E.M.S. (health, housing, education, employment, maintenance, and support). They also face restrictions on housing and where they can live, loss of voting rights, as well as requirements to report to parole officers and pay fees. Educational and employment opportunities are unattainable due to their inability to qualify for college admission under the Gainful Employment guidelines and get financial aid due to failed criminal background checks.

As the United States experienced an increase in drugs trafficked into the country from 1970 – 2015, America also experienced an increase in the Mexican population. In 1970, fewer than 1 million Mexican immigrants lived in the U.S.; by 2000, that number had grown to 9.8 million, and by 2007 it reached a peak of 12.5 million. A record 33.7 million Hispanics of Mexican origin resided in the United States in 2012, according to an analysis of Census Bureau data by Pew Research Center. This estimate includes 11.4 million immigrants born in Mexico and 22.3 million born in the U.S. who self-identified as Hispanics of Mexican origin.

According to the U.S. Census Bureau, in 1970 Blacks represented 11.4% of the US population. Twenty-two million Black people lived in the US. By 2000, that number increased to 36 million people. By 2010, "Blacks represented 14% of the total US population for a total of 42.0 million." "The total US population was 308.7 million as of April 1, 2010." The majority of blacks in America live in 10 states, mostly in the Southern states. This figure does not include an estimated 13 million aborted African American babies. On average, African American women terminate 1,876 pregnancies every day in the U.S. In 2014, the New York Post reported a decrease.

Millions of children in America have at least one parent in prison, and millions more are affected by the drug violence fueled by this country's demand for illicit drugs and the money it generates. Some of these children are orphans and wards of the state. Yet, drugs still remain plentiful in America, and the battle between government, demands for the pharmaceutical companies, and cartels who have set themselves up as independent governments to control drugs is responsible for poverty, mental illness, addiction, and death. Imprisoned persons cannot attain gainful employment, and children raised without parents are more likely to live in poverty, engage in delinquency, and drop out of school. These children also suffer from behavioral disorders and other mental illnesses. Turf embattlements stemming from the drug war ultimately lead to unnecessary deaths.

Anti-Drug Laws

The drug laws in America have always targeted the specific activities of certain groups based on race, religion, ethnicity, or nationality. Criminal laws against opium and cocaine targeted Chinese immigrants and Southern Blacks, respectively, and laws against marijuana targeted Mexicans. Cocaine was a legal drug in this country for many years. In fact, people could purchase cocaine from their nearest drug store. Due to its alleged curative powers, cocaine could be used to cure or aid against headaches, stomachs, and other body ailments. Laudanum (alcohol and morphine from opium) has a rich history as a palliative, and one of America's leading soft drink companies originally marketed it product as a patent medicine that contained an extract of the cocoa leaf.

Legislation enacted by Congress targeted specific drugs controlled by specific races or nationalities. The Shanghai Conference in 1909 controlled opium, Congress passed the Harrison Narcotic Act in 1914 (which, asserting its association with addiction, limited cocaine use to certain groups), and the Marijuana Tax Act in 1937 taxed Mexican imports to control the transportation and sale of marijuana. The United States also aided and financed the Russian Soviet–Afghan War until 1989 (the Afghans are the world's largest producers of heroin).

The past and current laws that govern the war on drugs in America include mandatory minimum sentences under the Boggs Act in 1951. Since the 1970s, the Rockefeller laws, mandatory minimums, R.I.C.O laws, C.C.E statutes, and 3-strikes laws have governed the war on drugs. In January 1973, former New York Governor Nelson Rockefeller announced the 'Rockefeller Drug Laws', but not before investing time, money, and resources in prevention and intervention programs like the Methadone program, which he believed failed.

Due in part to Rockefeller-style laws, the nation's prison population exploded from 330,000 in 1973 to a peak of 2.3 million by 2002; that meant building hundreds of new state and federal prisons. By 2010, more than 490,000 people were working as prison guards. The Rockefeller laws "created mandatory minimum sentences of 15 years to life for possession of four ounces of narcotics — about the same as a sentence for second-degree murder." These laws were enacted from the 1970s through 2004. Mandatory minimum sentences are sentences that apply to mostly drug offenses and are the minimum prison term length that must be completed before convicted persons can be released from prison.

In the late 1980s, the Reagan Administration enacted laws that created federal mandatory minimum drug sentences, federal sentencing guidelines (which also abolished federal parole and the unbridled discretion given to Article III judges in federal court), and a law creating a death penalty standard against 'kingpins', all under the Anti-Drug Abuse Act.

The Clinton Administration enacted the "3-Strikes" laws under the Violent Crime Control and Law Enforcement Act of 1994. The "Three Strikes statute provides for mandatory life imprisonment if a convicted felon has been convicted in federal court of a 'serious violent felony' and has two or more previous convictions in federal or state courts, at least one of which is a 'serious violent felony'."

The story of the Motor City Brothers is indicative of the impact of drugs, race, and class in America and the War on Drugs. To understand the life of two of America's Most Wanted, we have to discuss drug laws, the chronological history of Blacks in America from the 1960s through the New Millennium, and the Motor City Brothers' rise to fame and journey to the United States penitentiary. We'll also explore how they were victims of ineffective counsel.

Part One

1960 – 1970: PRAY OR BE PREY

One

Early Life in the Motor City and State of the Nation

"My argument against God was that the universe seemed so cruel and unjust. But how had I got this idea of just and unjust? A man does not call a line crooked unless he has some idea of a straight line. What was I comparing this universe with when I called it unjust?"
C.S. Lewis, *Mere Christianity*

Born to Robert and Shirley Johnson, David, Solomon, and their sister Suzanne endured the coldness of Detroit winters without heat, electricity, or food. Like many Blacks during the 1960s, their parents had a dream for a better life, and relocating from Cleveland to Detroit seemed to be the right idea. Detroit was home to the United States' automotive industry giants: Olds, Ford, Dodge, Buick, and Chrysler. It was also home to the man who founded Detroit, Antoine de la Mothe Cadillac, and the Cadillac automobile. Industry in Detroit was booming, as the Big 3 automotive giants made profits because Americans invested in their brands and products. Manufacturers produced vehicles that were opulent, reliable, and low-priced. By investing in American brands, people maintained employment and the working class was able to finance and provide for their families and support their schools and communities.

Formerly called Negroes, the term Black began taking on new meaning. Early life for the Johnson brothers was complicated by social, political, and economic forces. Faced with segregation, poverty, mass mob lynching, murders, and the rape of women and girls, Southern Blacks demanded equal rights. Students from across the country mobilized and helped lead the movement through the Congress of Racial Equality, Freedom Riders, the Student Non-Violent Coordinating Committee (SNCC), and multi-cultural church organizations. The civil rights movement reached new heights with the signing of the Civil Rights Act of 1964 and the Voting Rights Act of 1965. But while children in the south were integrated into white school districts and communities, northern states experienced unprecedented issues of poverty and housing discrimination.

James Baldwin wrote that the 1960s were turbulent times in America, saying,

> *"People who treat other people as less than human must not be surprised when the bread they have cast on the waters comes floating back to them, poisoned."*

During the 60s, the U.S. experienced the assassination of three of its most prominent political and social leaders: President Kennedy, Malcolm X, and Dr. Martin Luther King, Jr. As the Motor City belted out Motown's hits, like Freda Payne's *"Bring the Boys Home"*, Marvin Gaye's *"What's Going On"*, and *"Mercy Mercy Me"*, people still struggled to cope with the Vietnam War and the attack upon Black soldiers returning home to face discrimination and unemployment.

By the late 60s, several factors affected the Johnson home, the automotive industry, and life in Detroit. These factors included the demand for public and private unionization, the civil rights movement, transformation to an assembly line economy, and white flight. Blacks also found themselves unable to live in certain communities because of restrictive deeds and covenants prohibiting whites from selling or renting their properties to Blacks.

Two

War, Family, and Community and Social Reform

Writer Langston Hughes said in his poem "Beaumont to Detroit":

> *"Looky here, America*
> *What you done done--*
> *Let things drift*
> *Until the riots come."*

Faced with racial tension, police brutality, and the symptoms of social ills, the city experienced the riots of 1967, or the 12th Street riots, which began when police raided a local bar. President Lyndon B. Johnson ultimately sent in two airborne divisions to bring calm to the streets of Detroit, which had endured the loss of life and destruction of thousands of buildings. Nevertheless, trapped, confused, or living with foolish hope, Black people still had a love affair with the Motor City and the expectation to live a better life.

Some Blacks in Detroit lived as middle class citizens and enjoyed the luxuries of life. Detroit middle class families were well regarded nationally as the most thriving middle class sector of society, consisting of two-parent households led by well-educated, working class homeowners.

In the midst of this, the Johnson family faced an enduring problem of unemployment. The Motor City brothers had a painful spiritual journey from poverty to conquering ghetto life. Like many Black families, they were raised to have faith in God and believe He would supply all their needs; however, the family often had to rely on the other "G" — the government — to feed, clothe, and house them. Before welfare reform forced fathers out of the home as a compromise to helping families in need, people could get assistance. As children, the Johnson family relied on welfare benefits to pay its bills. Their father continued to struggle to maintain steady employment, and frustration from the fear associated with his inability to be a provider made him an abusive person. Like so many homes in America during the 1960s, the Johnson children witnessed domestic violence.

During the 1960s, almost 75% of Black men and women were married. Women of all races were victims of domestic violence. Some women did not have a voice in their homes and were treated like chattel. They relied on their spouses or significant others for more than moral support. For some women, the agenda of the time was to graduate high school, marry, and have children. Others pursued education and employment opportunities. Still, many were taught to be domestic and attend to their husbands and children. For Black women, the task was difficult; Black women had to balance work and maintain their homes.

Poet Nikki Giovanni shared the life of Black women in verse. Her interpretative writings revealed pain, suffering, and silent labor. She also wrote about Black awareness, unity, and solidarity, saying:

"There is always something to do.
There are hungry people to feed,
naked people to clothe,
sick people to comfort and make well."

While most middle class Caucasian women enjoyed the benefits of being homemakers and stay-at-home mothers with Black domestic help, Black women had to balance the roles of mother, wife, and worker - and the balancing act was not always enough for their mates. Some Black women experienced beatings and mental torment; however, maintaining an uncanny sense of loyalty for their men, they refused to prosecute because some Black men were experiencing the hell associated with being victims of uncontrollable circumstances associated with racism. There certainly was domestic violence back then, as women got their tails whooped and still were expected to give up tail, as well as cook, clean, and meet the needs of their spouses. Many did so with blackened eyes, broken noses, bruised or fractured ribs, and busted mouths with missing teeth. Perhaps some of the reasons they did not seek help were because most of their girlfriends and female relatives were also victims of domestic violence; the church was silent, and there existed no shelters for battered women, no support groups or victim programs. Nevertheless, police seldom addressed issues of abuse during the 1960s.

Like Shirley Johnson, Black women suffered in silence, the subjects of political, social, and economic forces. The women's movement and cries for equal rights did not extend too many benefits to their realities; nevertheless, Black women managed to maintain home, school, community, employment, and church life and did it all with a smile. They witnessed the struggles associated with the Vietnam War, discrimination, unemployment, drugs and alcohol, and their impact upon their home and community.

Poet Maya Angelou said:

"The need for change bulldozed a road down the center of my mind."
I Know Why the Caged Bird Sings (1969)

David and Solomon saw their share of abuse but never witnessed their parents using drugs or alcohol. They and their mother were subject to physical and verbal abuse, even though their father said he was Christian and loved God. The all-night physical fights between his parents made Solomon a very nervous child. Even in his youth, he felt obliged to defend his mother and would fight his dad to protect his mother. He vowed as a child never to hit girls but admits that he did adopt the verbal abusive trait of his father. David was a Mama's boy and could never do wrong, but Solomon defended her to the end. David and Solomon both experienced their fair share of discipline. Beaten like slaves, Mr. Johnson disrobed his children and used a belt to whoop them.

Back then, there was no 911, child abuse hotlines, or investigative authorities who challenged or interfered with parenting and disciplinary action. Teachers and people in the community observed children with marks and bruises and did not invoke the police or social workers or provide help. After all, Blacks were performing a learned behavior that passed down from slavery, the use of corporal punishment to tame their children was the method used by slave masters to tame their slaves.

Other than the verbal abuse, all-night fights, and having to fend off their father physically, David and Solomon enjoyed watching their sister and her friends jump Double Dutch, play hopscotch, and learn the latest dances; equally, they enjoyed sports, playing jacks, rolling dice, riding bikes, listening to music, or hanging out on the block. Their first stereo system and bikes were purchased from their local thrift store. Community was important, and everyone knew each other's families; like a village, their community was an extension of family and school that provided their children a safe haven to play.

The boys watched basketball and witnessed such National Basketball Association greats as Wilt Chamberlain, Bill Russell, Oscar Robertson, Walt Bellamy, Lenny Wilkens, Willis Reed, and Elgin Baylor. The athletes of the 60s were committed to their homes, schools, and community. For some, these men were heroes.

Without video games and computers, creativity among inner city children was the norm. Most children created their own street games like kick the can, in which the children stepped on a can, mashed the can on their foot, and kicked the can as far as it could go. Then, using the cap of the shaving cream can and filling it with clay, the brothers used to shoot the cap into the boxes of the hopscotch board; they enjoyed playing hide and seek, dodgeball, and a host of other games. Family game night and church were very important times, and Thursdays were always game night, when they played Pokeno, card games like Spades and Knuckles, and board games like Monopoly, Sorry, and the game of Life. When money or financial help from family members permitted, their summers and holidays consisted of block parties, barbeques, travel to their parents' hometown in Cleveland,

Ohio, and attending family reunions, where the elders of the family recited oral family histories.

Family time and church could not defend against the growing demand for drugs in Detroit. No matter how hard the Johnson parents tried to protect their children, the widespread impact of drugs began to consume their community. In the late 1960s, recreational drug use was widely consumed by young, white, middle class Americans; however, heroin use in the Black community was deadly and had an adverse impact upon the community. To address this epidemic, President Johnson's administration consolidated several drug agencies into the Justice Dept.'s Bureau of Narcotics and Dangerous Drugs (BNDD). In 1969, the U.S. government closed the Mexican border to prevent the smuggling of marijuana into the United States, and every vehicle entering the country was inspected for marijuana.

Part Two

1970 -1980: THROUGH THEIR EYES

Three

The War on Drugs and Family Matters

**"I can imagine having riches,
but my imagination cannot pay bills."
Sherri Jefferson**

Poverty was not the only enemy of the Johnson family; drugs within Detroit and around the country had an impact upon the lives of many Black servicemen returning home from Vietnam. In 1970, the Nixon administration passed the Racketeer Influenced and Corrupt Organizations Act (R.I.C.O), which focuses on racketeering that involves any act or threat, including money laundering, murder, kidnapping, gambling, arson, robbery, bribery, extortion, dealing in obscene matters, or dealing in a controlled substance or listed chemical and C.C.E. laws.

The Continuing Criminal Enterprise (CCE) statute punishes any person who engages in supervising, managing, leading, organizing or being an administrator or principal of a crime organization. CCE is also known as the 'Kingpin' statute and targets drug traffickers. At the time, the punishment of persons convicted to a mandatory minimum term of imprisonment was not less than 10 years, which may be up to life imprisonment.

Faced with a growing heroin epidemic among U.S. servicemen in Vietnam, in 1971 President Nixon declared a war on drugs. The Nixon Administration also created the Office of Drug Abuse Law Enforcement (ODALE) to establish task forces to handle drug dealing within cities across America.

While America waged a war on drugs, the Johnsons were causalities of the embattlement of poverty and political and social reform. The economy continued to impact the Johnson home. With the gas crisis, which began in the summer of 1972, and fears of continued shortages, consciousness of air pollution, and the inability to change manufacturing paradigms to compete on a level playing field with Japanese and European auto manufacturers, Detroit and its citizens suffered. Demands for equal pay and civil rights attributed to the enactment of employment and labor laws.

The women's feminist movement demanded equality among the sexes, but women like Ms. Johnson could not reject their homes to participate in the fight for women's rights. The feminist movement promoted 'pro-choice', the 1973 court decision of Roe v. Wade, and the legalization of abortions. Pro-choice gave a voice to everyone except the child. Genocidal services in the Black community focused upon ending the lives of Black babies through abortions, and less upon planning for parenthood.

Women's rights also meant employment opportunities and education. Black women understood that education meant liberation, and many pursued educational opportunities. Equal rights were as important to Black women as civil rights. Known as the "Mother of the ERA", Martha W. Griffiths, Michigan's own representative, sat at the helm of the passage of legislation for equal rights. Griffith committed her service to tax reform, civil rights, and the passage of the Equal Rights Amendment. In 1972, Shirley Chisholm, the first African American congresswoman, became the first major party African-American candidate to make a bid for the U.S. presidency when she ran for the Democratic nomination. She was also the first woman to run for the office of president of the United States.

Despite advancements for women, the Nixon Administration continued his war on drugs. In 1973, the United States created the Drug Enforcement Agency (DEA). In 1974, Detroit elected its first Black mayor, and later Motown left the Motor City for California. Drugs, gangs, poverty, and the tragedy of the public systems had devastated the city. Detroit had become the heartland of the American nightmare. Political power did not transform into economic or social advancement, as poor Blacks remained stuck in Detroit, surrounded by affluent white suburban communities.

The Johnson parents continued to create a safe haven for their children, still pushing for education, church, and a village community. By the mid 1970s, David and Solomon had attended school, engaged in community activities, and spent a great deal of time after school watching television shows like The Jeffersons, the Brady Bunch, Flintstones, Dennis the Menace, the Jetsons, and Good Times. House parties were very popular, and it was no different in their home. Mr. Johnson would host family and friends on Saturday night for pot-luck dinners, where people brought a dish and shared food, good times, and music by Aretha Franklin, the O'Jays, the Temptations, and Kool and the Gang. They did not engage in the use of illicit drugs or alcohol. When food was plentiful, Sunday dinners consisted of fried chicken, baked macaroni and cheese, candied yams, corn bread and greens. Ms. Shirley, as their mother was affectionately called, was a great cook. The family also watched television programs on Sunday nights. The NFL played on their TV screen on Sunday nights, after Mickey Mouse and the Disney programs.

When the Johnson boys became of age, David began to DJ for profit. For recreation, he used to breakdance; however, Solomon had two left feet. Despite all their efforts, there were many days with no electricity, no water, no heat, and not enough food. The brothers obviously could not concentrate in school and did not graduate. Solomon spent most days too scared to leave the house because he feared he would miss his mom getting beat. He also suffered academically because he focused so much on her abuse that he could not concentrate during school. Finally, his mother gained enough courage to get a divorce, but his parents remained together, and even after the divorce they went to church together. The children were confused by the nature of their parents' relationship, and their confusion would manifest later in life.

David and Solomon had childhood friends whose hopes and aspirations included becoming the mayor of Detroit, and other friends whose paths and dreams were misguided and who would eventually go to prison: Mike, Roy, and Stick. The brothers dated, had female friends, and were sexually active by 14 and 15 years of age, respectively.

Four

Politics and Fast Food or Fast Money

After years of experiencing and living a life of poverty, which included threats of eviction and displacement, the Johnson brothers made the decision to pray or be prey: make fast food or make fast money. Like so many young men before them between the ages of 12 and 25, the lure of selling drugs to escape the battles of poverty is inevitable, and it is the reason for the poverty-to-prison pipeline. Too young to weigh the long-term collateral consequences associated with the value of freedom, they resolved to make fast money because their choices were very limited. Praying meant continuously relying on a God who had never answered their prayers and allowed them to continue to remain in poverty. To be prey meant they had to be victims of their circumstances and suffer. What God allows His people to suffer on Earth with an imaginary belief that an afterlife in a place called Heaven is better? Such a thought makes a person content with living in hell, hoping to find solace in death.

The scriptures suggest that faith without works is dead, meaning people must be expected to apply their faith to change their circumstances. Perhaps with or without God, the end results will be the same. By now, the Johnson brothers witnessed the effects of the deadly Ds: drugs, drunkenness, debt, death, divorce, destruction, division, and disease, as men returning from Vietnam were dying from Agent Orange and drug related deaths. They saw men suffer alcohol and mental illnesses. They witnessed their communities suffer from the post-war decline in marriage and its effect upon the state of the Black family; therefore, it was easy for the brothers to think they had a better chance of changing their circumstances than sitting and praying to God for an unknown result.

Sure, they believed in God, but not as most. They believed life was an illusion and that the imagery of life is created by the person living it. In their minds, destiny is not created by some unknown God, but by the person traveling the journey. They refused to submit to the idea of wait-and-see. They recognized early in life that God had not answered their prayers and that prayers absent action meant nothing. It was only when they acted on their faith that tomorrow possessed a better day.

So they made a decision: they decided they would act, not react, to their suffering by finding a way to change their financial circumstances without malice, intentional harm, or violence. So without having to rob or kill someone, they resolved to learn how to make money to help their family maintain the basic necessities of life: food, water, and shelter in a country whose promise is life, liberty, and the pursuit of happiness.

Although God had not directly answered a specific prayer, they believed He would protect them because He knew their hearts were set upon being providers for their family. Their decision to assist their parents was a biblically sound decision to honor their mother and father. The brothers' opportunities were based on capitalism, the law of supply and demand (basic economics), the fundamental need to provide the basic necessities of life, and the ability to live the 'American Dream'. Clearly, in pursuing the American Dream, they became the most wanted Black family in America.

Meanwhile, the government continued its war on drugs. In 1978, the Comprehensive Drug Abuse Prevention and Control Act was amended to authorize law enforcement to seize all money and personal and real property of persons involved in dealing drugs. Although most laws purported the goal of prevention, the goal has always been to control the flow of drugs.

Part Three

1980 -1990: MADE IN DETROIT

Five

Making of D-Money and Cali, Drugs in America

"I did not create this world; I just occupy space. If I were
God, there would be no such thing as the devil, debt,
disease, divorce, drugs, drunkenness,
destruction, division or death."
Sherri Jefferson

Like most youth living in urban communities, David and
Solomon witnessed white flight from the inner city and the
relocation of jobs to the suburbs. They also lived through the
decline of the automotive industry and the struggles
associated with the dismantling of the Bell
Telecommunication System and anti-trust regulations. These
variables, plus the union and labor issues, were part of the
disappearance of the middle class and the creation of a new
America: The Rich and the Poor. These changes were readily
seen in the Motor City.

Detroit, now a city completely divided by race, economics,
and politics, was ruled by drugs, gangs, and a declined
economy. From being able to cash out to people paying car
notes and mortgages, from being KO'd to no longer being best
friends, the streets devoured young boys. No longer able to
create an economy, Detroit became an urban warfare where a
judgment could not be delivered from chambers.

By now, the government had grown accustomed to enforcing its policies on its so-called War on Drugs. Initially, drug use in America was considered nothing more than a form of political opposition, challenges to social reform, and an act of rebellion. But endemic to Blacks, the inner city, and the poor, they saw more and more militarization of the police and violation of their 4th Amendment rights. The so-called War on Drugs soon became a war against addiction, and addicts were the enemies in the war on drugs. The purported War on Drugs also became a war against targeted groups and their communities. Blacks and Latinos became prisoners of war and suffered from the arbitrary and discriminatory enforcement of federal and state legislation under R.I.C.O. (Racketeer Influenced and Corrupt Organizations Act), C.C.E. (Continuing Criminal Enterprise), Rockefeller laws, and mandatory minimum sentencing laws.

David and Solomon were made in Detroit, and their trials and tribulations prepared them for survival. And while the CIA was allegedly *funding the Iran-Contra operations by exporting cocaine to the United States through "Freeway Rick" -- Ricky Donnell Ross, then a Southern California drug dealer* -- Americans were influenced by a multi-million dollars "Just Say No" to drugs campaign by President Ronald Reagan and his wife, Nancy Reagan. But the Johnson brothers, without a marketing budget, convinced people to say "yes" to the purchase of cannabis. They possessed marketing skills, and like preachers, they had charismatic gifts.

Six

Black Culture and
Make Money or Make a Difference

The 1980s was a guiding force for David and Solomon. The period represented two worlds that influenced Black America. Politics, sports, social reform, and music were the first world. The Apartheid movement in South Africa, Angela Y. Davis' *Women, Race & Class*, and rap music by New Yorkers Chuck D, Kool Moe D, KRS One, Afrika Bambaataa, Grandmaster Flash and the Furious Five, and Doug E. Fresh were symbolic of the times. Not to be silenced, female artists MC Lyte, Ms. Melodie, Queen Latifah, and Monie Love delivered messages of empowerment. Tairrie B. (Theresa Beth), the 'Wicked Witch' of the west, inspired rappers.

David and Solomon spent many evenings watching the bad boys of the NBA; Detroit's own Isaiah Thomas and John Salley were sports figures and contributors to their communities. The NBA's Earvin "Magic" Johnson, Dominique "Human Highlight Film" Wilkins, Danny Ainge, and Larry Bird also gave back to their communities. The NFL and MLB athletes who contributed to their communities were Michael Irvin, Deion Sanders, and Barry Sanders, to name a few. These athletes represented a new breed of players who entered multi-million dollar contracts. Their salaries were often the topic of discussions on college campuses, mainstream media, and in social circles by many who felt Black athletes made too much money.

A long way from the stereotypes of movies like "Super Fly", "The Mack", and "Cotton Comes to Harlem", Spike Lee's "School Daze" revealed the issues of classism within Black America, and "The Cosby Show", "A Different World", and the "Oprah Winfrey Show" ruled the 1980s. Although the 80s represented a drastic decline in Black marriages, it also saw an increase in the enrollment of Black men and women in colleges and universities, despite overwhelming obstacles. The U.S. Small Business Administration and venture capitalists issued public grants and private funding to female, Black-owned and operated businesses; consequently, Blacks saw their largest increase in business ownership since the 1920s and 1940s.

Conversely, like many Blacks, David and Solomon were influenced by BET and MTV. The Crips, Bloods, Gangster Disciples, Vice Lords, and Pirus mastered the mental, then a new set of gangsters emerged in the 1980s - studio gangsters - who created Gangsta Rap music. This was the beginning of a lost generation whose lives were stolen by life sentences. Black men soon fell victim to the streets as the gangs and music industry introduced America to an interesting concept of the term "nigger". The term took on a new meaning (nigga, niggaz, and niggah), and its abusive exploitation was portrayed in film, videos, and music.

The dichotomy of NWA and NWB is that NWA's composition evolved around First Amendment rights, a reflection of reality for some Black males involving police brutality and the invasion of drugs in the community and their impact. It is indisputable that the group had one of the industry's best music producers and one of its best writers and lyricists. By contrast, NWA is also NWB, who introduced Blacks to mainstream America as "Niggas, Whores, Bitches".

Music and videos depicted Black girls and women as negative stereotypes, suggesting they were gold digging, unemployed, uneducated bitches and whores seeking to be upgraded by any means necessary. No other race has before or since publically berated and disgraced its women as these Black men did, and these depictions and stereotypes sent Black females back to slavery. The FBI, Congress, the media, and the music industry did not censor their lyrics until they targeted members of law enforcement and white people.

My nigga, yo niggas, those niggaz
It's a shame
Took the word and gave it fame
The lynches, the vote, the back of the bus
Civil rights leaders never made a fuss

The word has history
From slavery to bravery
The misguided sold their soul
Stories left untold

Justifiable homicide
No crime committed
You a nigger, so it's permitted
Lifetime of change since Reconstruction
Continue to engage in self-destruction

The gangsta rap views represented misogynists who believed Black women and girls could not control their sexuality or bodies. It also represented the views of men with personal issues involving self-esteem, masculinity, and unresolved

46

issues from relationships with their mothers and other female figures; nevertheless, these negative views played into the long held stereotypes of mainstream America that Black women had worked so hard to dispel.

The truth is that Black women will work and maintain a job *rather* than give a job; however, unlike women of other races, Black women have been forced to carry the world on their shoulders because some of their men fail to meet their responsibilities to family and community. Therefore, like women of any race, ethnicity, or nationality, Black women will do whatever it takes to support themselves and their families. Remember, it was Black men who introduced these Black women to drugs and a life of prostitution. Many girls and young women were trafficked, strung out on drugs, and forced to find the means to support themselves or feed their children.

Like many Black Americans during the 1980s, David and Solomon observed the impact of HIV/AIDS. HIV/AIDS emerged in inner city America as the government banned funding for syringe access programs to prevent the spread of HIV/AIDS during drug use. Originally alleged to be a gay disease, HIV/AIDS also emerged in the Black community from Black men being on the down-low, and from men who engaged in survival sex during prison incarceration, then returned to their communities resuming a heterosexual lifestyle.

Prison rapes and sodomy had these men living morally indecent. The acts of rape and sodomy caused these men to live like animals, unable to control their sexual desires. Officials released men into their communities, never informing the public that they had contracted HIV/AIDS during their incarceration.

By 1986, life was darker than death. Crack cocaine had impacted inner city America; the death of an NBA draftee from a cocaine overdose and the birth of crack babies forced the nation to finally take a stand against drugs. It was too late as babies born to mothers with an addiction to crack had to experience withdrawal. Some mothers delivered stillborn babies. Many mothers lost custody of their children at birth, and others were subject to arrest for the drug charge of possession of crack by digestion. Other mothers were forced to give birth to their children in leg shackles because they tested positive for crack cocaine, and after delivery they would be charged and jailed.

However, America did not declare crack addiction as a mental health issue, and it treated crack addicts as criminals by creating a drug bill. The Reagan administration enacted the Anti-Drug Abuse Act of 1988 and allocated $97 million to build new prisons and created mandatory minimum criminal penalties for drug offenses which sentenced persons to serve ten years in prison. Discrimination in the differences in sentencing for crack vs. powder cocaine was endemic to Blacks, Latinos, and the poor.

Overzealous law enforcement and prosecutors engaged in misconduct, using informants to aid in the arrest, charge, and prosecution of innocent people; many were charged as co-defendants and co-conspirators. Many of these victims lived in federal or state housing developments also referred to as 'Projects.' The real *project* is an agenda to create an environment of future criminal offenders. The projects house underserved and economically challenged people in apartment complexes with prison bars on their windows, front doors made of steel and elevators doors like the cell block. The playgrounds resemble a prison yard. They are surrounded by militarized police and urban warfare.

Sadly, many informants informed against innocent, poor people who went to prison because they were financially unable to defend against their charges, and they were afraid of challenging their charges because, if unsuccessful, they could face longer prison terms, which included mandatory minimum prison terms and no parole. Many of the defendants were under the age of 25 and faced ten and twenty-year mandatory minimum sentences. Crack cocaine and criminal prosecution with long prison sentences are tools of urban warfare. America's shame.

New player on the block
Representing hip hop
Liquid platinum in the streets
Powerful, stopping heartbeats

Liquid dollars, abuse of power
More potent than heroin and smack
Tools of war, America under attack

Strung out stillborn, another lost life
Strung out husband and wife
Mothers and daughters, victims of the street
Children starving, no food to eat

No law or order
Depiction of evictions and convictions
Dilapidated buildings and penal institutions
Violations of the Constitution

Failed public education
Can't excel
No money for bail, so wait in jail
Mandatory minimum incarceration
No treatment, no rehabilitation
No wills, no insurance, nothing to pass on
Homeboys dead, buried and gone

Meanwhile, Congress, Black politicians, and local community advocates were actively seeking to make people the targets of their unfortunate circumstances with disparate impact and sentencing laws for base cocaine (crack cocaine). These laws sentenced people to longer prison terms than for the use of powder cocaine. Casualties of the fatalities of urban warfare, the streets had devoured Black babies, and Blacks lost many young men and women. No longer caregivers of their community, the two worlds of Black America collided. The 80s was the beginning of the tyranny of the foster care system, juvenile detention, and the implementation of the court system serving as a surrogate for Black children.

Impoverished, hungry, unemployed, and victims of political, social and economic discrimination, the Johnson brothers, like many people, tried to create their own economy, mainly by making a name for themselves by selling cannabis at $50 per sack; the mantra *Get Rich or Die Tryin'* could hardly be attainable from this premise. David, aka "D-Money", and Solomon, aka "Cali", had a plan, but in the meantime selling cannabis came with a price. D-Money's girlfriend was shot and killed in Michigan. Later he met a young lady who would mother his child, but the love of his life was gone, and he would never be the same again. He refocused his attention on his business. He closed his heart to other options and continued that journey.

On the other hand, Cali had three special women in his life. Rebecca was the love of his life and mother of his children. Then he maintained a relationship with Samantha, but she was an older, married woman with children from two other men. Both of her men were low-level drug dealers and known snitches. She told him she had divorced.

Samantha introduced Cali to the night life: clubs, partying, etc.; compared to most, he was a homebody. During their relationship, Cali got shot 5 times on 3 different incidents. The first one was a jack move in 1986, by someone trying to rob Cali; the 2nd time was a hit in retaliation for taking over the hood for selling cannabis. Some old cats were not fond of their movement. They shot at D-Money as well, and during that shooting Cali sustained an injury to his eye. Even back then, people said they had a lot of heart, and the police said they had done them a favor by running the old men off the blocks.

Some of the cops were crooks back then, too. One may understand why; the average police officers in America's inner cities are paid less than $50,000 per year to man operations against drugs in their zones or precincts. These officers observe young Caucasian, Asian, Latinos, and Black males driving expensive vehicles, living lavish lifestyles, owning stately homes, and dressed to the nines; so it is not hard to understand why some police officers will take cuts from their collars or why they will rob drug dealers. Moreover, it is not hard to understand why some officers will falsify their monetary collection reports from an arrest or why they will work for the dealers by running other dealers off the block and subjecting them to arrest. It is not difficult to understand why some police officers will steal drugs from dealers or confiscate from dealers or their own evidence rooms. Law enforcement agencies recover billions of dollars in drug money, but the money benefits everyone except the police. These abuses lead to police brutality, unjustifiable homicide, and the refusal of some police to respect or protect minority communities.

Most of the monetary recoveries from drug busts do not purchase new vehicles, anti-drug operations and equipment, weaponry, bulletproof vests, or specialized helmets. The recoveries are not used toward life insurance policies or increased salaries. In fact, the life of a police officer in America is insured for less than the cost of a luxury vehicle, at a policy rate of $100,000 or less. Compare that to the cost of a Bentley, Aston Martin, Maybach, or a Range Rover. People on the streets of America are starving like in third world countries. Honor, dignity, and pride are not sufficient principles to die for in the war on drugs. It is no wonder why the suicide rate of 18.1% for law enforcement personnel is higher than the 11.4% in the general population. Policing the battlefields in the war on drugs in America is a difficult task. In many instances, police officers are outnumbered, unprepared, and underpaid when faced with real drug traffickers. It is much wiser to join dealers than work against them.

We question why some communities in urban America lack police presence and patrol? No police were present during any of the attacks against Cali or D-Money. The streets were barren. During the last shooting, Cali inadvertently jumped in the middle of a turf war. The shooting involved Keisha's brother and his homies from around the way; she was one of Cali's female companions. The shooting immediately stopped when they realized Cali got hit. A street war is a war without terms; it is an endless war with many battles. Should you fear danger or mystery? One is seen, and the other is unseen. So as the cliché goes, selling cannabis on the streets of Detroit would come with dangers.

The night Cali got shot, Samantha was sneaking around with her "ex-husband". So Keisha nursed him back to good health, as well as the mistress of the former mayor of Detroit. Following the shooting, he required surgery and was a victim of medical malpractice and a very lucrative financial settlement. Soon, the brothers from the Motor City were the embodiments of the American Dream; the proceeds from the settlement secured them a future as America's most wanted Black family. The brothers financed legal business ventures: a taxi cab company and restaurant. This venture took the brothers from collision to progress.

The lack of business and employment opportunities fuels crime, violence, and illicit drug use in inner city communities like the Motor City. When the Johnson brothers reinvested in their community with their taxi service, they not only filled the void of providing transportation, they also offered employment opportunities to members of their community. Hailing a cab ride in any inner city community is stressful. Many minority communities experience acts of discrimination simply trying to get a taxi ride. So this investment was driven by their desire to give their community a well-needed, deserved service that provided affordable, reliable, and trustworthy transportation. At the same time, they employed people from the community.

Although the restaurant and taxi cab company began to prosper, the Johnson brothers continued to supplement their income by selling cannabis. Alcoholism, depression, and unemployment plagued many Detroiters, and like 655 people arrested in Detroit between 1987 and 1988, D-Money experienced his first encounter with the system in 1988 for possession of drugs and received a sentence of two years on probation. He happened to visit Atlanta, and shortly thereafter the brothers left the Motor City for a better life in Atlanta and California. In 1990, they departed from Michigan, never to live there again.

Part Four

1990 – New Millennium: ALL IN THE FAMILY

Seven

From East to West, Economics and Politics

"Loyalty is more than a word; it is a lifestyle."
Cali

Fake ass with 'make it rain' riches; wigs, weaves, tits, tats, rats, and snitches - Welcome to Atlanta!

Was the move to Atlanta one the Johnson brothers would live to regret? What do you really know about the *dirty south* or its *southern hospitality*? What do you really know about *ridin' dirty*? What do you know about *rats* who eat through bricks?

With proceeds from the restaurant and taxi company (which were generated from the lawsuit settlement), the brothers purchased a condo in Atlanta; soon after, their world changed. They faced different challenges from when they resided in the Motor City. Some of those challenges included defining themselves in a southern city. The Johnson brothers expected the South to be a little slower in terms of pop culture as compared to northern cities, but they were taken aback by the slave mentality of some who lived in fear of retribution. Disturbed by people who constantly reminded them of the stories of sharecropping, chain gangs, and the civil rights movement, the brothers expressed that Atlanta and the state of Georgia were not the only people who faced injustice.

Factually, the civil rights activities like the March on Washington, Selma, and other events took place in other states. Dr. King lived in Alabama, and everything from the bus boycott to the fight to vote happened on their soil. Black people from all over suffered from oppression.

The Johnson brothers envisioned Atlanta as the Mecca of the South, the home of Black consciousness and operators of the visionary Dr. Martin Luther King, Jr. They perceived Atlanta as a progressive city of unity and solidarity; however, they soon realized Atlanta was very divisive and the Blacks living there suffered from classism. The Black natives had two worlds of haves and have-nots. The first time D-Money heard the term "old money" was during a conversation with a young lady who professed that her family represented the "old money" in Atlanta; old money represented professionals and business owners who lived in the Cascade, Benjamin E. Mayes, and Peyton Road areas.

The complexities of the different lifestyles amongst Black people in Atlanta were disappointing. Cali had no idea Atlanta had so many impoverished areas, like Bankhead Highway and the various housing projects. He could not envision that the home of Dr. Martin Luther King, Jr., suffered from poverty and had areas where people lived in shacks akin to third world countries. Although not a historian or economist, D-Money still questioned how the Atlanta University system, which is the largest consortium of historically Black colleges - including Spelman and Morehouse - surrounds housing projects, low-income housing, and poverty.

The Johnson brothers had a moral compass and were very surprised Atlanta had so many strip clubs where girls danced for a living. This compass explains why D-Money initially gave so much money to dancers and why "make it rain" became his anthem. Initially, he wanted to ensure that these girls had financial resources to help finance their cost of living.

In 1989 and 1990, Atlanta was developing its brand. The Georgia Tech football team had a successful season, The Real Deal had won the heavyweight title, and their baseball team won the national championship (although the owners traded their Black pitcher and dismantled the winning team immediately thereafter). Meanwhile, Red Dog roamed the streets of Atlanta, seeking whomever they could devour. The night life in Atlanta was thriving, with clubs like Dominique, Club Deion, Club 131, Diamonds and Pearls, Rupert's, Club 112, and for the Southside goers Mr. V's and Markos was banging. Atlanta hosted Freaknik as the Black college community enjoyed spring break. The Magic City strip club was a hot-spot venue for Black strippers, while Cheaters and Pink Pony were frequented by white patrons seeking white strippers. Unbeknownst at the time, the stripper scene in Atlanta would prove to be fatal.

If the 80s represented the NWA, then the 90s surely defined SWA – Sistas with Ambition! Mary J. Blige, Erykah Badu, Lauryn Hill, Whitney and Toni Braxton taught women how to escape from life's problems. Hip Hop artists Li'l Kim and Foxxy Brown redefined the role of females, and their lyrics promoted a life of *"female, fee-male, and free-male"*. The 90s allowed some women to master the art of *giving* brain, while others obtained a college degree for *using* their brain, everyone made a profit. Trying to *escape* the negative stereotypes of the 1980s, the 90s represented the beginning of the Black female experience and their struggle to overcome the negative stereotypes deployed against them through gangsta rap music, film, and video. Black women were eagerly pursuing their ambitious goals, and education, employment, homeownership, and entrepreneurship were the bare essentials.

The women in Atlanta who migrated from out of state brought these essentials to the south, and their blend of northern assertiveness, mixed with southern hospitality and mannerism, served them well. The bona fide southern belle met the newcomers with reservation but would come to terms with their neighbors by sharing their way of life and learning from one another. Being very reserved, Cali preferred *around the way* women and maintained his relationships with northern women, but D-Money refused to discriminate, knowing he could never replace his one true Michigan love.

Blacks were now called African Americans, and the country was at war in the Middle East. Atlanta had submitted its bid for the 1996 Olympics and hoped for a state lottery program. African Americans and whites still lived separate and unequal lives. For example, in the late 80s early 90s, most African American Atlantans lived on the south side of town, in areas like Campbellton Road, Cascade and Peyton Road, and areas called the SWATS. Others lived in College Park and Old National.

The 1990s represented the beginning of gentrification in Atlanta and other cities across America; it's a form of reverse white flight, where instead of people moving to the suburbs, many families demand to live within the city limits. Areas once grimly neglected are now recipients of corporate investment funds and federal government subsidies for renovation. The 90s was the beginning of the demolition of the Atlanta Housing Projects. Some families were evicted from public housing based on allegations of drugs, criminal records, and accusations of violating ordinances. Many families from Capitol Homes, East Lake Meadows, Perry Homes, Bowen Homes, and Herndon Homes were victims of displacement. Most of those communities were part of the gentrification and became commercial or residential condominiums, townhomes, and single family homes. The displaced families could never afford to live in those communities. Section 8 vouchers financed moves to the suburban communities within the Metro Atlanta area. Many families were unwelcomed, and their children were victims of the school-to-prison pipeline, special education classes, and disparities in school discipline measures.

Like the brothers from the Motor City, most migrants frequently moved to Buckhead, in Atlanta, or Marietta, Georgia. DeKalb County was still facing white flight in the early 90s, leaving behind stately properties D-Money knew he would own one day.

The 90s represented social reform in music, movies, and entertainment. Movies like *House Party* and *Boyz n the Hood* portrayed the lives of two different types of inner city youth. Comical, one portrayed the lives of two young middle class suburban kids; the other reflects the lives of impoverished males raised in single parent homes. Movies and music became cutting-edge.

From *Tigger in tha Basement* to one of the greatest lyrical beefs in rap history between Jay-Z and Nas to radio play, the Black music culture had entered a new era. From Jack the Rapper conventions to Bronner Brothers' hair show, Atlanta developed a reputation for music and entertainment. Not to be outdone, Detroit hip hop artists were ever present and regularly came through Atlanta in their iconic style of full length fur coats with matching hats, luxury cars, Adidas sneakers with track pants, and jewelry. Meanwhile, Michigan's Fab 5 controlled NCAA basketball and set new athletic standards and fashion trends.

Entrepreneurship was on the rise, and many Black artists went from one mic to writing, producing, directing videos, and label ownership. They relied on the larger labels for distribution.

The Motor City Brothers had amassed wealth from their own business ventures and became sought after by music industry executives for the use of their homes, cars – including their Bentley – jewelry, and access to yachts and a Learjet. These material possessions are displayed in many videos from the 1990s. Imagery was important to establishing a brand in the music industry and gaining and retaining consumers. D-Money had given great consideration to entering the industry as the owner of a label. He had always loved music, and his gift of DJing and marketing parties in the early days had proven profitable. Atlanta was the ideal city to start a record label. At the time, there were only two labels, both catered to a southern hip hop genre. Other labels were developing their brands as imprints of larger record companies. While hip hop artists and their labels benefitted from the use of the Johnson brothers' possessions or access to luxury items, many did not entertain D-Money's ideas for starting his own label. Since the Johnson brothers were not about disturbing the peace, they continued to manage their other affairs. While D-Money was a business person, he did not have experience as an A & R, and he lacked experience in creative sponsorships, performance and artist development, and product marketing and publicity.

Nevertheless, the brothers continued to thrive. D-Money and Cali did not acquire fame and fortune from selling the roc. The brothers became cash money millionaires from other ventures. They were living the American Dream with the motto that the sky is no limit. D-Money and Cali premised their business upon loyalty, integrity, dignity, honesty, and brotherly love. They were bad boys, but they were not rough riders or ruthless. The brothers never committed murder or put anyone on death row. They reaped from the aftermath of Cali's shooting, which led to a medical malpractice lawsuit. Using those proceeds, they had a promising future involving no shady business and no crisscross. Some people were so deceptive, but D-Money and Cali continued to be young, fly, flashy, and honorable. Men of fortitude, the Motor City Brothers proved that *loyalty is not a word, but a lifestyle.*

Meanwhile, Cali had decided to relocate to the west coast. He had set his sights on the land of fruits and nuts, guns and roses. When he arrived in California, drugs, HIV/AIDS, gentrification, crack cocaine, and gang violence plagued the city of Los Angeles. The East and West coast rappers engaged in lyrical battles. The Crips and Bloods and the 18th Street Gang and Mara Salvatrucha (aka MS-13) ruled the streets. The L.A. police department had a very hostile relationship with African American and Mexican youth and their communities. Employment opportunities for young men were scarce. California also offered 3-Strikes legislation, which punished third time felony offenders under Prop 184, Penal Code 1192.7, to serve 20 years to life imprisonment upon conviction of their third offense. Nevertheless, through his lens, California offered him a great place to raise his children and be with Samantha. Cali loved the west coast and had no intentions of returning to either Michigan or Atlanta.

By now, he and D-Money lived separate and different lives. Cali enjoyed evenings listening to Anita Baker and watching Arsenio Hall. He enjoyed jazz & R&B, and the only rappers he listened to were Prophet, Lyricist City, and the King of New York. He had established a great working relationship with members of the community. Cali settled in Bel Air and became a member of one of the most well-known churches in California. The congregation included members of the business community, as well as local, state and federal law enforcement agencies and prosecutors. Several members represented their political districts. He knew everyone, and he became a respected businessman for his ventures in the community.

Meanwhile, his home life was great. At the time, he and Samantha appeared to have it all. One day Cali had a conversation with his landscaper, and that conversation would forever change his life. Through his conversation, he developed a connection on rebuilding cars, and this would prove profitable for his new venture. He entered one of the most lucrative businesses in California that targeted diverse communities: drag racing, cruising, and pimping rides. From Northern California to Southern Cal, whether in Los Angeles, Ventura Beach, Compton, Long Beach, or El Dorado Hills, drag racing, pimping, and cruising remained the most frequented activities or events in California. The stakes were high, and the investments were profitable. This was an excellent investment opportunity for Cali, and he accepted the challenge. He opened several businesses that offered services to the drag racing, pimping, and cruising communities. Cali and Samantha co-managed their ventures, and the businesses grew to be very profitable.

The mid-90s was historical. African Americans demanded Ebonics as an acceptable language. How did they go from slaves learning to read and write by candlelight to an African American presidential candidate pushing an Ebonics curriculum? In the midst, 1995, 1996, and 1997 took the lives of three of the most revered and major rap artists in America's history. The rappers represented the Westside as victims of the streets. Married days before his death on March 26, 1995, 'Simple' allegedly died from AIDS complications. It appeared that neither the wife, mother of his children, nor children had HIV/AIDS complications. The *life of boyz in da hood*.

Surpassing the 1963 March on Washington, on October 16, 1995, a million Black men gathered for the Million Man March on Washington, a gathering for justice and reform. The leader of the March, Minister Louis Farrakhan, organized the march with a message of unity, family, and economics. He instructed the participants to return to their families and rebuild, restructure, and redefine their priorities to confront issues plaguing the Black community.

On August 15, 1996, the 'Prophet' attended the Brotherhood Crusade along with his label owner and Charlie Brown, Sledge, and others. This crusade challenged California's Civil Rights Initiative (CCRI), also known as Prop 209. Prophet, Charlie Brown, singer the Dream, and others agreed to participate in the fundraiser to bankroll their political agenda. It would be the first use of his image to address a political agenda. He went as far as to say he would be a different man come the year 2000 and he desired the establishment of a new political party. He entered *thugz mansion* on September 7, 1996, less than two weeks before the fundraiser.

On March 9, 1997, a shooting ended the life of East coast autobiographic 'Lyricist City'. A purported composite sketch of a suspect exists, but the person supposedly remains at large. *Who Shot Ya?*

The 1990s marked a decade riddled by music, social reform, and politics. The 42nd President of the United States, the Clinton Administration enacted, enforced, and enhanced criminal laws which included mandatory minimums and 3-Strikes laws. The administration continued to ban federal funding for the needle exchange programs that would help prevent the spread of HIV/AIDS. His administration also passed the *welfare to nowhere* program, where poor women went from no pay, to low pay, to struggling everyday just to make a way; all in an effort to end reliance upon public assistance and welfare for private citizens. Meanwhile, corporations received billons in government assistance and aid (welfare/public assistance). The North American Free Trade Agreement was a failed program and law that sent American jobs overseas. The U.S. Sentencing Commission acknowledged the racial disparities in cocaine vs. crack sentencing and recommended eliminating mandatory minimum sentencing and sentencing disparities, "**but for the first time in history, Congress overrode their recommendation.**" Clinton's Administration refused to end or stop the sentencing of people to mandatory minimum prison terms. The prison cycle continued. America's shame.

Finally, just as America failed to respond in a timely fashion to the Jewish Holocaust, where 6 million Jews were murdered; America sat silent while Africans were murdered

65

in a Rwandan genocide, a holocaust involving the mass murder of children and women by Tutsi and Hutu tribes.

Part Five

New Millennium – 2008:
AMERICA'S MOST WANTED

Eight

Voices from Within

"We share everything...we can't take this shit with us."
D-Money

Several Atlanta artists exhibited skills in the art of rap. A businessman, D-Money invested in their talent. He purchased studio recording and production time, he created promotional music videos, and he distributed smack DVDs and CDs. By 1999, he had invested in the careers of Baby Cake, Mr. Intellect, and Frozen. D-Money also invested in the career of an artist from the West coast named the Code. He brought another cat named Wall Street from the coast to Atlanta. Coincidentally, as soon as he began working with these people, a national tip hotline opened, and some joined the Sunday morning breakfast club eating bacon, cheese eggs, and grits. Like toddlers in high chairs, each spilled a bowl of grits. The local, state, and federal agents gained access to private video footage, photos, telephone conversations, addresses of private residences, attendance at private events and nightclubs, etc.

In the interim, D-Money's local acts became a force to be reckoned with. He started DMJ Entertainment and entered the music industry. D-Money used his initials DMJ to name his entertainment company, then DMJ posted a billboard with his initials in Atlanta with a slogan from a popular 1980s movie. Like other music executives of that time, he also used slogans based on iconic Americans from organized crime families. It was a marketing ploy that helped promote his brand. In hindsight, D-Money's initials gave it an air of criminality; however, he operated a legitimate music and publishing company. His sole intent for the use of the three letters was to promote future hip hop artists like Frozen and Code by using a brand people could identify with.

As the entertainment company expanded, so did the entourage of local acts. Thereafter, people were wearing the DMJ moniker on their hats, clothing, and jewelry. Like with any group, some people became uncontrollable. Many members of the entourage conducted themselves in a disorderly manner and were accused of being associated as a gang. However, DMJ was never a gang within any meaning; it is not an accurate depiction of the family. It was a group of local artists and their associates. People associated with the company from a distance began engaging in acts that were not known or condoned by D-Money. Their actions brought negative attention to his company.

By now, D-Money had controlled several mansions, including The Rocket Ship, The District, and Lizzie Taylor, although Samantha was the legal owner because of her relationship with Cali and her ability to manage business and financial affairs. Nevertheless, D-Money hosted several musical promotion parties at The Rocket Ship and The District. The grand residences were located in the affluent communities of Fulton and DeKalb counties. DMJ lived a lavish lifestyle, and he freely shared his wealth because, he said, *"We can't take this shit with us."*

While the internal warfare between BGF and the MM spilled from prison to the streets, the new millennium brought new people into D-Money's life, and his success brought new problems. While Voices from Within claimed they would 'Go hard or go home' and 'Death before dishonor,' in 2001, as America faced a threat to its national security, unbeknownst to D-Money, hidden voices had plotted against his life. From 2001 to 2003, as his music company produced top talent, he poured himself into his artists and producers. By 2003, the company, which included a magazine division, had built their brand locally and nationally, with the artists selling DVDs and performing in venues and surrounding states.

During 2001–2003, Cali remained on the west coast. He continued the successful operation of his business of providing services to participants in the pimping, cruising, and drag racing community. Business flourished, and in 2003 he purchased a 2004 F-150, 2004 Bentley Continental GT, 2003 Suzuki Street Motorcycle, 2004 Street Motorcycle, and a 2004 Infiniti QX56. D-Money had his own fleet, which included a Ferrari, Bentley, and Lamborghini.

Finally, the brothers from the Motor City were enjoying the fruits of their labor. Then, lions, tigers and bears – oh my! From a lavish 36th birthday party in June to the burglary of his accountant's home in September 2003, D-Money's future looked grim. Like most businesses, D-Money and Cali leased luxury vehicles for tax benefits. On some occasions, Xecutive Brands of Atlanta sold vehicles to them. Mr. Information, the owner of Xecutive Brands of Atlanta, hired Mr. Sunset to assist in selling vehicles; unbeknownst to him, Mr. Sunset was a local police officer who reported to authorities that Xecutive Brands had been using straw borrowers to purchase luxury vehicles for suspicious clients. Mr. Sunset tried to extort Mr.

Information for payments to remain silent concerning his investigation, but Mr. Information refused to give him any money.

Soon thereafter, on September 7, 2003, someone burglarized Mr. Information's home in Atlanta. He shot and killed the burglar, and he reported the shooting. When the police arrived, they were granted access to other areas of the townhome unrelated to the shooting or burglary. Inside the townhome, the police found one kilo of cocaine and a bank-size safe. Ironically, on behalf of the police department, Mr. Sunset obtained a search warrant of the home, claiming the homeowner possessed information about illegal car purchases and leases for local drug dealers. The search revealed documents with information about the purchase of vehicles, but it did not name or implicate D-Money or Cali.

There is still suspicion that the burglary was staged by local police officer Mr. Sunset to get the police into Mr. Information's home. It is no coincidence that the burglary of the townhome occurred after Mr. Information refused to pay Sunset in exchange for withholding information about Xecutive. There is still suspicion that Mr. Information's cooperation was bought by offering immunity to another major client. There is also still suspicion that the entire police operation was targeted at D-Money, even though there was no evidence of any wrongdoing by D-Money, DMJ, or Cali, and certainly nothing that would have justified an indictment.

Mr. Intellect shared similar troubles with D-Money, because every time he tried to move forward with his career, Voices from Within incriminated him, and he continued to get arrested, violate parole or probation, and eventually served time. These jealous acts thwarted his career.

Then on November 11, 2003, chaos marked the beginning of a nationwide investigation into D-Money, DMJ, and Cali's affairs. There was a full moon on 11/11 when Puck, aka 40-caliber, and Sanford, aka 380, were victims of a double murder. Native Bronx New Yorkers, Puck and Sanford were very well known and respected by music industry executives. In 1994, they relocated to Atlanta with their families.

Puck and Sanford were childhood friends. Victims of an 11/11, a double homicide, their deaths were the remarkable simultaneous occurrence of an event. Earlier that day, Puck returned to Atlanta from Miami with a foot injury. Puck had attended a birthday celebration for his longtime friend in the music industry. D-Money also attended the party.

Later that evening, Puck and Sanford hung out at the Buckhead club and went home. Puck received a telephone call suggesting that he return to the club. When he arrived, Puck saw his cut, Rahab, who was entertaining with D-Money. An argument ensued, and Puck was removed from the club. Initially, he went home. However, he received another telephone call and returned back to the club. He waited around the area, and gunshots were fired; he and Sanford sustained multiple gunshot wounds. Their homicides ignited a cry for change in Atlanta's nightlife. The Buckhead community demanded that night clubs close earlier, more police presence, and more cameras in the community.

After the shooting, Voices from Within began speaking. Rahab reported that she saw D-Money fire seven bullets on that evening; fortunately for Puck, in January 2003 he dedicated his life to God and his one prayer was that he would never die in the streets or beyond the wall. It appears God answered his prayer, because he passed away at a local hospital. Authorities were unable to recover video footage from street cameras or locate a firearm or any other corroborating witnesses to the shooting. Furthermore, D-Money had been shot in his buttocks. He said he'd heard gunshots and ran. His injury would suggest he was running away from the direction of the firing of the bullets. He immediately called Cali to convey that he had been shot and was headed to get medical attention. He sought medical attention at Richland General Hospital, north of Atlanta. Cali was with Keisha that night and had no knowledge of the events leading up to the shooting.

D-Money was not a violent person and had no prior history of violence. The 11/11, double homicide, was unfortunate and regrettable. Death is final, and there is no coming back from it. Long-time associates of D-Money have long said he did not want to associate himself with violence or death; however, it seems forces outside of his control conspired to bring both of those to him.

Surprisingly, Mr. Sunset obtained another search warrant following the murders of Puck and Sanford, and he searched 'The District'. During that investigation, he recovered firearms, a business card belonging to Cali, money counters, and documents connecting Mr. Information and Xecutive Brands with D-Money. The documents revealed the purchasing of vehicles and telephones, but no criminality. The telephone records linked associates of D-Money and Cali to the Purifier crew in Detroit.

The DEA was investigating the Purifier crew. On the contrary, D-Money and Cali were not under DEA investigation in 2003; only local authorities and the FBI were investigating information about the brothers based on hidden voices in Atlanta. Members of the Purifier crew were indicted and arrested. Secret voices told stories of links between D-Money and Cali. The DEA expressed an interest in the stories and opened an official investigation. Now D-Money and Cali were under investigation by the elite forces of the DEA, FBI, CIA, and HIDTA.

In the meantime, local police arrested D-Money on charges of double homicide. He paid a one-million-dollar bail. Later, the ballistics testing of the firearms proved that guns belonging to D-Money were not used in the murders of Puck and Sanford. D-Money was not a felon and could possess a firearm. As law enforcement continued their investigation, they learned one of the persons linked to the Purifier Crew, D-Money, and Cali was related to a mayor in Georgia. Upon concluding their investigation, whispering voices provided information concerning the scope of D-Money and Cali's business ventures.

D-Money's future looked bleak. He found comfort in spending special evenings with Molly, while unbeknownst to him people he trusted were sharing incriminating information with law enforcement. The government said Voices from Within were fully and truthfully cooperating witnesses who qualified for a downward modification of their federal sentence or were immune from prosecution without any court proceedings. These sentencing provisions are less than mandatory minimum sentences.

Voices from Within shared incriminating information about Cali to law enforcement. The device used to wiretap his cell phone could only be placed by someone who had access to the phone. The secret voices grew louder and could be heard from coast to coast. D-Money went to Florida, and Voices from Within told authorities of his whereabouts.

Thereafter, the hidden voices made allegations about the brothers, which included that they had established an international cocaine distribution network, with cells in Pineview, GA, and throughout the United States in cities like Detroit, St. Louis, Atlanta, Los Angeles, Miami, and Dallas. They were accused of establishing two main hubs for their alleged operation. Voices from Within claimed the brothers operated from an Atlanta, Georgia, hub for distribution, and a Los Angeles, California, hub which allegedly operated incoming shipments from Mexico.

Although law enforcement investigated those allegations, no evidence or wrongdoing was uncovered – no drugs, no drug money, no trafficking, no crimes at all. The secret voices suggested law enforcement reconsider traffic stops from 1994–1999; law enforcement reinvestigated traffic stops recovering hundreds of thousands of dollars. To that point, no one from those stops had ever implicated the brothers. Again, it appeared D-Money and Cali had successfully overcome accusations of being drug traffickers.

But Voices from Within were lyrically gifted. It was no longer a gangster party, because jealousy and envy became enemies of D-Money and Cali. There is a difference between the greed and violence of crime and the simple jealousy and envy of people for those who are successful, regardless of whether that success comes from real or illegal activities. The simple truth is that D-Money had associated himself with people who had inwardly yearned for and envied his transition into the music industry. At the time, his financial success threatened many in the industry. Somehow, the Voices from Within became louder and more lyrical. No one escapes the target of America's elite forces: the DEA, FBI, CIA, and HIDTA.

Thereafter, D-Money and Cali's fates were sealed as two of America's Most Wanted. Sad but true, their adversaries were haters of the game, and angry, as they lacked the skills to share the profits from the name. Shootings were allegedly linked to the Johnson brothers, but they never managed, organized, supervised, led, or administered any killings. The FBI tried to bring the brothers from the Motor City to "justice", but the agency's attempts were thwarted due to lack of evidence.

As early as December 2003, Voices from Within included low-level criminals who bargained successfully for reduced sentences, immunity, or dropped charges in return for their cooperation or testimony against the Motor City Brothers, even though law enforcement was initially unable to corroborate any of the accusations. Field offices in Michigan, Georgia, Florida, the Carolinas, Texas, Missouri, and California worked diligently to secure indictments.

While local and federal agents and authorities wasted taxpayer dollars to monitor the activities of D-Money and Cali, in search of an international drug trafficking enterprise, victims of child sexual exploitation and slavery and girls not old enough to drink could legally strip off their clothes for intoxicated grown men. D-Money and Cali's challenges were small in comparison to the challenges faced by other

Georgians. Georgia's new law set the stage for underage strip dancing, and thereafter drugs were not the only things trafficked through Atlanta.

In Atlanta and across America, children as young as 10 years old, mostly African Americans, were prostituted. African American men pimped and trafficked underage girls to white "johns" and organizers of the pornography industry. Human trafficking is genocidal, destroying the lives of women and girls, and it is more deadly than the alleged drug trafficking activities of D-Money and Cali; unfortunately, federal authorities never shifted their obsession with indicting and arresting D-Money and Cali to identifying, locating, and prosecuting other people responsible for trafficking humans.

But life goes on, and as the girls were told they could be famous, Atlanta's strip club scene advanced. Being licensed to dance at Strikes, Club Touch, and the Man Clave became a requirement. Then on July 25, 2004, people saw red like the delicious cake. '8th Floor' shot and killed a man outside of a club in Atlanta. '8th Floor' was an associate of D-Money; however, D-Money was not present at the shooting and had no connection to the deceased. It appeared the shooting may have followed an evening of drinking. When the men exited the club and entered their cars, the deceased allegedly gestured to let the driver of the car know he was walking behind it; not wanting to be struck by the car, he would be struck by bullets. Two people were actually struck. One person died from the senseless shooting.

Now the federal agents had the information necessary to work toward attaining indictments; however, most of the information was based on lies, entrapment, and false reports of monetary returns and collections. Still, America's elitist forces stormed into several states seeking indictments.

While the District Attorney's office explored criminal charges against associates of D-Money, the office was also presented with information about teachers in Atlanta Public Schools system and their involvement in a cheating scandal. The D.A.'s office was prosecuting the shooting death of a judge and deputy sheriff. The APS scandal soon became a federal and state case because it demonstrated some of the problems associated with teachers in urban school settings, which included unprofessional teachers and administrators struggling with classroom management, inability to successfully perform lesson and unit planning, and meeting academic demands. These problems extended to addressing disciplinary matters, as well as the inability to prepare students for standardized tests, which entitled teachers to financial benefits based on their passage rates.

On June 16, 2005, law enforcement officials captured the mayor's relative; trouble for D-Money and Cali lurked around the corner. Hurricane Katrina was not the only natural disaster of 2005 that displaced African Americans and left people without money, food, and material possessions. As America's elitist forces stormed into several states seeking indictments, by October 2005 the well went dry for everyone. D-Money and Cali were arrested in Texas and Missouri. D-Money was arrested at his residence in Texas after a female companion called authorities and reported his whereabouts. A hidden voice had already leaked his whereabouts days earlier.

Cali was arrested in Missouri after a Voice from Within called and reported his whereabouts. Some members of DMJ and persons associated with D-Money and Cali thought the brothers would leave the country. Feeling abandoned, Voices from Within became impatient when they or their loved ones had been arrested and unable to communicate with the brothers to get bail and bond out of jail. Facing the inevitable, the brothers hired attorneys for their associates and tried to secure money for families before they faced arrest. *Loyalty is more than a word; it is a lifestyle.*

Under surveillance the brothers did not have full access to their accounts. From hidden voices to visible people, law enforcement obtained information leading to the arrest of D-Money and Cali without incident. At the time of arrest, the Johnson brothers did not possess firearms, drugs, or money to substantiate their being leaders of an international drug ring. There was also no evidence that established either of the brothers was the administrator or principal of the acts leading up to the July 25, 2004 shooting or any financial collections from drug traffic stops.

Nine

Fact or Pulp Fiction

"We the last ones left...only God can judge me now."
Tupac Shakur

For more than a decade, people have said David and Solomon were kingpins who had forged an alliance with the Mexican Cartels. Americans should be inclined to ask how many kingpins exist at one time in the United States. If the brothers were kingpins, then who are Larry Vacuum, Chris the Soft Drink, Racecar Driver, Sim *Red* Card, Super Bowl, Vegas, The Court, Baby Face, August the Bird, Sal Magazine, Rose Gardens, Purifiers, and Mohammad, to name a few? Without a legal definition of the term kingpin, individuals are subject to the arbitrary and discriminatory enforcement of criminal laws that lead to life in prison without parole, or pine box sentences.

At the same time the government alleged that the Johnson brothers were kingpins controlling drugs in the streets of America, they indicted other alleged kingpins. According to the DEA, on July 13, 2005, a grand jury sitting in the Eastern District of Michigan at Detroit returned an indictment charging 23 individuals with various drug trafficking and money laundering offenses. Twenty-two of those individuals were charged with conspiracy to distribute marijuana and cocaine and money laundering, in the Detroit area and

80

elsewhere, from 1994 through 2005. The indictment also charged defendant Larry David Quincy with operating a continuing criminal enterprise involving the distribution of marijuana and cocaine in Michigan, California, Arizona, Colorado, and elsewhere. Quincy was alleged to be the principal supervisor of the enterprise that is charged with the distribution of more than 30,000 kilograms of marijuana, which generated illegal drug proceeds well in excess of $10 million. He also faced life imprisonment[1] and a $178-million-dollar judgment. In February 2011, the feds revealed the arrest of four Atlanta men, and in July 2011 they said the use of a wiretap helped their agencies convict Red, a Louisville man, for his participation in DMJ syndicate. Red was convicted for moving 100 bricks a month.

In September 2013, members of the United States Senate met to discuss mandatory minimum prison terms, and during the hearings someone asked about the definition of a kingpin. There exists no legal definition of a kingpin in the United States. There also exists no definition that explains how much drugs must be sold or managed before a person is called a kingpin. There exists no specific dollar amount of drugs to be sold or a specified period of time before a person is called a kingpin.

Drug manufacturing and distribution is the equivalent of engaging in the unauthorized practice of dispensing drugs and pharmaceutical services. In most jurisdictions in America, the unauthorized practice of law and medicine are misdemeanors punishable by no more than twelve months in jail. A person can perform surgery on an individual, be prosecuted for the unauthorized practice of medicine, and not

---

[1] http://www.dea.gov/pubs/states/newsrel/detroit072005.html

be sentenced to mandatory minimum sentences of 20 or thirty years; however, the penalty for the unauthorized practice of dispensing drugs and manufacturing drugs is up to life imprisonment or the death penalty. The War on Drugs is premised upon hypocrisy and corruption and has led to 7.3 million imprisoned Americans since its inception.

You hear the names The JAG, Mr. Columbian, or Brotherly Love, and immediately you associate their names with alleged drug trafficking and a connection to South America, Central America, or Mexico. The story of the Johnson brothers plays no differently. In making their case against David and Solomon Johnson, law enforcement officials alleged they were connected to the Brotherly Love Cartel. The Brotherly Love Cartel was five brothers from Mexico. Authorities claimed these brothers were engaged in the business of manufacturing and transporting cocaine, heroin, and marijuana. Mexican cartel ranks include the Free and Sovereign State and the "Z". Until 2014, Brotherly Love forged alliances with The Zs.

The most lucrative cartels worldwide include the Medal Cartel, the Juan Cartel, and the California Cartel, and if the statement of a United States presidential candidate has any merit, then we know no American can enter the world of drug trafficking without permission from the CIA or the cartels. Drug trafficking is "a gold mine for people who want to raise money in the underground government in order to finance projects they can't get legitimately. It is very clear that the CIA has been very much involved with drug dealings," Ron Paul said[2]. Toward that end, the role of the Mexican cartel in the transportation of cocaine, heroin and marijuana is not farfetched. However, upon closer review, there is no evidence

---

[2] http://www.huffingtonpost.com/2011/12/30/ron-paul-conspiracy-theory-cia-drug-traffickers_n_1176103.html

of any direct connection between the Johnson brothers and the cartel.

Law enforcement claims that Race Car, a drug wholesaler, and Brotherly Love had a relationship. Race Car, aka Kansas, is an African American male who was born in Tennessee. He was raised in the Riverview–Kansas neighborhood by a hard working mother who laid a spiritual foundation. Religion played a critical role in his life; nevertheless, Race Car dropped out of high school and started dealing drugs at 19. He met a member of Brotherly Love, Mr. Mattel. Over the years, Race Car developed his trade and market. After years of dealing drugs, Race Car began developing trade routes, which included travel to Mexico. Purportedly using overnight courier services and 18 wheel trucks, he crossed the U.S. border with millions of dollars in drugs and cash. Race Car's success involved his ability to use communications codes that were only decoded by use of letters and numbers. Wherever possible, his crew never used the telephone, and when necessary, they changed telephones immediately after usage.

Race Car managed drugs in Tennessee, Michigan, Mississippi, North Carolina, Texas, Georgia, and several other states. He owned several homes, possessed a fleet of cars, and had millions of dollars in cash. In 2002, indicted by a grand jury with Vee-Jay and Trucker, Race Car faced prison for possession and distribution of 600 pounds of marijuana, and he fled to Mexico. While law enforcement alleged that Race Car eluded arrest, it is clear he availed himself to his crew, because he continued to conduct meetings with his lieutenants, Trucker, Greenleaf, 42nd, and handlers. In August 2004, the U.S. Marshals added him to their 15 Most Wanted list. Race Car continued to maintain residency in Mexico, in a community called Milenio III, and everyone knew he was there. But law enforcement took four additional years to make an arrest.

Mexican authorities arrested Race Car in Queretaro, Mexico, on Jan. 10, 2008, and he was the subject of seven sealed indictments that included allegations of murders. Because the government seized his assets, Race Car, like many accused American drug dealers, was denied access to money to hire a legal defense of his choice. He received a court appointed attorney, a government employee.

David and Solomon Johnson entered their plea in November 2007, and in September 2008 the court sentenced them to thirty years in prison. Contrary to all the hype and misstatements, the United States elite forces of the DEA, FBI, CIA, and task force never conducted a two-decade investigation into the affairs of the Johnson brothers or DMJ. The Johnson brothers did not plead guilty to federal drugs charges; they pled guilty to money laundering, as the underlying felony of the CCE.

Following his arrest in 2008, Race Car was listed as a cooperating witness for the government, but he never implicated DMJ or the Johnson brothers as drug traffickers or having had any association with the Mexican cartels. The government made several attempts to uncover the cartel's drug and trade routes; the government learned that there exist more than 500,000 commercial flights, that over 5 million people travel by sea or ocean liners, and that there exist in excess of 100 million vehicles and over 80,000 merchant passengers' ships, with excess of 7 million shipping containers and over 100,000 small vessels. They learned that drugs travel through the Central America–Mexico Corridor and drugs enter the U.S. from the Jamaica Maritime methods to Canada, Europe, New York, Boston, New Jersey, and Miami, Florida, within the USA.

In December 2009, the government convicted Race Car. He entered a plea, and a federal judge sentenced him to nine life terms without parole in federal prison. His conviction included allegations of drug trafficking and murder charges. He appealed his conviction, claiming he had worked with the feds as a cooperating witness. He lost his appeal because the government said he did not cooperate. He never implicated the Johnson brothers or alleged their involvement with Brotherly Love.

Ten

Empire State of Mind

"Shining like new money."
D-Money

The Johnson brothers are visionaries who had the audacity to think big. Visionaries build great companies and forge alliances. They are dedicated and dependable people with the ability to overcome obstacles, be accountable and responsible for their actions and others, and motivate and develop people. The brothers from the Motor City possess a set of values developed through childhood and adolescence that served them well in their adult years. These values included loyalty, honor, integrity, and the love of family.

As visionaries, David and Solomon had confidence, loved life, and enjoyed people. They worked and played hard but were compassionate about others. Candid and fearless, the brothers said what they meant and meant what they said; they asked for forgiveness, but not permission. Possessed with emotional intelligence, these brothers were logical thinkers who were question-oriented, but solution driven. David and Solomon were not conformists, but they understood that followers become great visionaries. Visionaries do not manage, organize, or supervise; they are not administrators or principals.

Can the government hold the brothers vicariously liable for the alleged acts of people in their surroundings? Can they lead, manage, supervise, or organize independent contractors? As the founder of DMJ, David contracted other people to provide services, but those people were not his employees. The Johnson brothers did not control the acts of any contractors or their job performance. No evidence exists of any payments made by David and Solomon to anyone. The brothers never paid for any expenses or reimbursed anyone for cars, housing, gas, food, telephones, tools, or supplies. Finally, there are no written contracts or evidence of employee type benefits.

David and Solomon's attorneys failed to establish that the government must weigh all these factors when determining whether a worker is an employee or independent contractor for prosecution under CCE. Like a Japanese management blueprint, the emphasis is on the need for information to flow from the bottom of the company to the top; however, there is no evidence that information flowed in any direction. There were no hands-on activities involving the brothers from the Motor City. All purported telephone calls never connected David or Solomon to drugs, drug money, seizures, violence, or trafficking.

Their business operation included a successful taxi cab company, music enterprise, and magazine. Through these ventures, the brothers from the Motor City gave birth to a family of entrepreneurs around the country. The Motor City Brothers redefined the meaning of capitalism, family and business, and hoodology and urbanology. It was in their DNA that these brothers would possess the knowledge, skills, and have the foundation and cornerstones to be great businessmen. A successful business requires a high degree of formalization, operating leverage, and the ability to embrace autonomy. Business schools across the globe make millions of dollars to educate students in the art of business; corporations spend millions in salaries to fulfill the positions of CEO and CFO, with hopes of hiring men like the Johnson brothers.

David and Solomon's travels from the Motor City south to Atlanta and west to California led the government to ask how one family, a Black family, controlled the streets of America. The United States government indicted almost 150 entrepreneurs, but none of the eight indictments or the convictions against David and Solomon involved the distribution of drugs, possession with intent, a violent offense, or murder.

Although the Johnson brothers were successful businessmen, they were not attorneys. Therefore, they became victims of ineffective assistance of counsel. Today, David "D-Money" Johnson and Solomon "Cali" Johnson endure the harshness of serving 30 years in prison. Nevertheless, they know they are innocent as accused; they stand on their founding principles of Death before Dishonor for Life! They'd rather die in prison like men than live on the streets like cowards. Are they the last ones left? Surely, they are more than legends of the street.

40 dollars and change
Empire state of mind
Poverty-to-prison pipeline
Camouflaged in all black
Fell asleep before the attack
Make it rain riches
Streets got cats living like bitches
Like a savage for the cabbage

Doctors, scientists, and lawyers live on the block
Three hots and a cot
30-year pine box
No shots
Hard living for the American Dream
Do they understand what we say or care to know what we mean?
The block has the future of America in its hands
Waiting on love from Uncle Sam

Part Six

2009 – Present: AMERICA'S SHAME

Eleven

Scales of Injustice

"The Constitution is what makes America great."
Sherri Jefferson

Victims of ineffective counsel, David and Solomon's attorneys failed to provide adequate legal representation.

In 2005, the brothers were arrested, detained, and denied bond. At the time, the United States had policies that grossly interfered with the legal representation of defendants accused of drug trafficking. The government seized more than a dozen residences located in Georgia and California, more than three dozen vehicles, and almost $5 million in cash. The government's policies interfere with a defendant's right to retain an attorney of choice. The policies also subject attorneys accepting payment for a legal defense to criminal charges under money laundering laws. In the United States, every person who is accused of a crime is presumed innocent until proven guilty by the government.

Some of the legal deficiencies in representation include the fact that no plea negotiations had been sought to depart from the mandatory minimum or secure sentencing under RICO for the underlying offense of money laundering, as opposed to CCE conviction. Their lawyers never filed objections to the presentencing report. Their attorneys did not adhere to any professional norms, despite their representations, and if they'd known the attorneys had ignored these material factors, the Johnson brothers would not have pled guilty. The brothers have always maintained their innocence of the charges in the indictment.

In a press release addressing adults deprived of effective assistance of counsel in Pennsylvania, the Attorney General of the United States said, "For too many public defenders, crushing caseloads and scarce resources make it impossible to adequately represent clients who need and deserve assistance in legal matters. The Constitution of the United States guarantees adequate counsel for indigent defendants, and the Department of Justice is committed to ensuring that right is met. The Sixth Amendment right to counsel requires more than the mere appointment of a member of the bar. . .the right of indigent criminal defendants to an attorney may be violated by the government's actual denial of counsel or by a constructive denial of counsel."

Prisoner Denial to Pacers or Access to Court Records

David and Solomon remained incarcerated from 2005 to 2008, awaiting trial, and were held in the Sanilac County Jail, located at 65 North Elk Street in Sandusky, Michigan. The facility did not provide inmates with Pacer or Internet access, thereby denying them access to their case file. Further, the brothers were first-time felony offenders and had no knowledge of case file research or understanding how to interpret court files and records.

It may be hard to understand how two brothers from the Motor City could be victims. However, once you are detained and deprived of your liberty, your life is in the hands of an attorney, judge, and jailers. You do not have access to computers and court files. If everyone you know, including your father, is incarcerated, then who can help? Next, consider that during their two-year pre-trial detainment, they were denied access to their case files because the county detention centers did not have any electronic access to their court filings. Like most people, when you are subject to legal representation, you presume your lawyers are doing what they are paid to do or commit to do; you expect them to effectively and ethically represent your interest.

Bond/Bail

Every person is entitled to a bail or bond hearing under the Eighth Amendment. Both brothers were denied bond from 2005 and remained incarcerated awaiting trial until 2007; the court sentenced the brothers in 2008. The record lacks evidence establishing that either attorney demanded a bond hearing after the initial denial.

Mr. Salmon appeared in court for Solomon in October 2005 and initially represented him. Solomon's lawyer received five hundred thousand ($500,000) dollars in cash for bond, and David's lawyer received one million dollars, because David felt that due to the Atlanta incidents, his bail would be higher. David and Solomon did not receive bond. Their lawyers did not refund their money. In fact, Mr. Salmon ceased communications with Cali and literally abandoned the case.

Over a three-year period from 2005 through 2008, only one motion to secure bond had been filed after the original one, and that motion was filed more than a year later.

Wiretaps

Then there are the troubling issues concerning the court files, which prove that the brothers were the subject of ineffective assistance of counsel. Many people assumed that the case was over before it started because of alleged "wiretaps". The wiretaps allegedly consist of conversations with persons to include Solomon and the use of "drug codes" during those conversations; however, his lawyer never challenged the government to prove the existence of drug codes.

Under a federal rule of law, an attorney is authorized to have the Court conduct an evidentiary hearing on the issue of a wiretap. First to determine whether the wiretap is authorized or permitted by law or in violation of constitutional rights, then to determine whether the person accused is the person on the wiretap, then to determine the authenticity of the wiretap and the recordings. In their case, neither lawyer filed a motion seeking to prove whether the person on any of the wiretaps was Solomon. Respectfully, just because the government attorneys say they have evidence, it does not mean members of law enforcement legally and ethically secured the evidence.

The crux of the Michigan case rests largely upon nine (9) purported intercepted calls, which if proven false would not subject either brother to an indictment or to Michigan's jurisdiction. The record lacks any evidence to prove the lawyers filed several motions important to the outcome of the case. They did not file a Frank's motion, a Motion to Suppress Evidence of Illegal Wiretapping under Title III, and there is no motion under 901, 704, or 701 that could identify the voice or establish the identity of the parties to the telephone calls. The courts have expressed great danger of unfair prejudice in allowing expert testimony to offer an opinion about drug code words in a narcotics transaction.

Discovery and Plea Negotiations

Their attorneys did not request "Discovery". Discovery is the information secured by the State or Government consisting of evidence that is to be used against the accused in a criminal or civil case. Both sides share this information so they may prepare their case or trial strategy. It is clear their lawyers misrepresented the existence of evidence in the record or on file in the case.

Another problem is that their attorneys failed to conduct examinations or take depositions of government witnesses, depose witnesses, and verify the accuracy or the validity of the government's $270,000,000 money judgment. Their lawyers failed to investigate and present substantial mitigating evidence at the punishment phase. Counsel failed to engage in plea bargaining through a use of assets, restitution, fines, and the departure from mandatory minimums under CCE, or to seek to sentence under R.I.C.O.

Challenges to the Indictments

The record in their case also establishes that neither attorney challenged several police seizures or money confiscated from October 1996, October 1997, September 1999, October 2001, January 2001, March 16, 2004, or 2005 traffic stops. What happened to the collections? None of the attorneys deposed the alleged drivers, the police officers, or other witnesses involved in these alleged traffic stops to question their role in the stops, their communications with the alleged drivers of vehicles, or whether the dollar amounts in question were accurate collections or if there was a connection to the Johnson brothers.

The indictment fails to establish David and Solomon, individually or in concert, engaged in a continuing criminal enterprise. The attorneys failed to examine the elements of continuing criminal enterprise to determine whether the government could satisfy each element. For example, the indictment clearly states that the alleged criminal activity transpired since high school in 1990 through 2005; however, it fails to demonstrate any evidence of "continuing" criminal activity from 1990 to 1994 and alleges isolated incidents that include one from 1996, 1997, 1999 and two in 2001, with no evidence of continuing illegal activities. There were no alleged activities from 2001 to 2003. And in 2004, the brothers are only accused of nine (9) telephone calls purportedly made over a six-day period by Solomon. However, none of the calls are proven as drug transactions or money laundering.

Pre-trial Forfeiture

The excessive fines clause also authorizes the civil and criminal forfeiture of property seized during or as a result of drug raids or activity; however, their attorneys failed to challenge the federal drug forfeiture statute because it does not authorize an exemption for assets to be used for legal representation consistent with the Fifth and Sixth Amendments. Even where an attorney may lose such an argument, the attorney must act with due diligence and zealous advocacy.

The Court denied the Johnson brothers due process because nearly every circuit court of appeals requires an adversarial pre-trial evidentiary hearing before depriving a defendant of the assets necessary to afford counsel of their choosing. The denial is a violation of Constitutional rights unless prosecutors can show before (emphasis added) the forfeiture that the evidence supporting an indictment justifies the seizure of those assets.

Post-Forfeitures

And it is not over yet, because in violation of the 14th Amendment Due Process Clause, Solomon did not receive notification of the forfeiture against property where he had an interest. The government knew he was incarcerated in either the county or the U.S. penitentiary. Service of process of notice upon inmates who are subject to forfeiture via a newspaper publication is not sufficient legal notice. Inmates do not have access to receiving or reviewing the notice. Furthermore, the posting of the notice at a local courthouse when they are in prison is not legal sufficient notice; therefore, the following items were subject to forfeiture or seizure in violation of the law because Solomon could not challenge his interest in the property.

Vehicles:
Mr. Johnson purchased and legally owned the vehicles. The vehicles were seized from his property and were in his possession, custody, and controlled at the time of the seizure. Mr. Johnson did not receive any notification of forfeiture pertaining to these properties.

> 1) 2004 F-150 was administratively forfeited. No party filed a claim to this vehicle.
> 2) 2004 Bentley Continental GT was administratively forfeited. No party filed a claim to this vehicle.

3) 2003 Suzuki Street Motorcycle was administratively forfeited. No party filed a claim to this vehicle.
4) 2004 Street Motorcycle was administratively forfeited. No party filed a claim to this vehicle.
5) 2004 Infiniti QX56 was administratively forfeited. No party filed a claim to this vehicle.

Bank Accounts:
Mr. Johnson's property in Woodland Hills, CA, with Ms. Cummings possessed the money seized from his business and personal accounts maintained under her name or his business entity. Excluded from the list of proceeds includes $560,000 named in the indictment that was seized from his property in Woodland Hills, and $1,868,759 the government claims belonged to Mr. Johnson from Woodland Hills, CA.

1) $159,851.30 seized from Bank
2) $157.46 seized from Bank

Jewelry:
1) Assorted jewelry seized from Frisco, Texas, was administratively forfeited on June 5, 2007. No party filed a claim to this jewelry.
2) Assorted jewelry seized from Bel Air, California, was administratively forfeited on August 18, 2007. No party filed a claim to this jewelry. Plus, there was a post-indictment seizure of property belonging to Solomon from a jewelry shop in California.

Another issue is that the attorneys failed to proffer any evidence in support of Solomon's legal business enterprise, which he established with legal proceeds from the medical malpractice lawsuit. Furthermore, the attorneys never presented any evidence on his behalf that proved he had actual or constructive ownership, control, or possession of the vehicles stopped by police.

The forfeiture problems include that the property located in Woodland Hills allegedly had $1,868,759 in cash (a very odd amount of money). The indictment states that Mr. Solomon Johnson owned the vehicles, property, and currency. The government relied on this information to bring criminal charges. The collections are a far cry from $10 million. How could the government substantiate the forfeiture status of the currency?

The biggest question is, where is the money? The indictment alleges that $1.1 million dollars was in bank accounts that were seized in 2005; however, the government forfeiture documents filed in Court allege that only $159,000 and $57.95 were in those accounts. The grand jury considered inaccurate information to issue an indictment. The information fails to prove the "substantial income" element of the CCE statute. Alternatively, the lawyers should have challenged the funds - $1.8 million and $1.1 million - that were removed from these accounts before the Court authorized forfeitures.

Constitutional Challenges to CCE

The language of 21 U.S.C. § 848 is confusing, vague, and ambiguous because the statute is subject to more than one meaning. For example, the statute says (A) . . . "which are undertaken by such person in concert with five or more other persons with respect to whom such person occupies a position of organizer, a supervisory position, or any other position of management. . .." and further says in (B) . . . "from which such person obtains substantial income or resources. . ."

The crux of the issues rests upon two arguable questions. Did the judicial interpretations of §848 under the Continuing Criminal Enterprise statute provide the Johnson brothers fair notice and prevent arbitrary enforcement? Second, can a Court properly interpret §848 now to provide fair notice to future defendants and prevent future arbitrary enforcement?

Because the brothers can contend that §848 is vague and ambiguous, then let us focus on the second question, because respectfully, the evidence establishes that neither the grand jury, the prosecutor, the Johnson attorneys nor the Court had a sufficient interpretation of section 848 when David and Solomon were indicted in 2005.

Under the doctrine of constitutional avoidance, a Court must determine whether it can interpret §848 to provide the constitutionally sufficient definiteness that Congress failed to include in the language of the statute. The answer is no. The Supreme Court has held that "[L]egislatures and not courts should define criminal activity." And that "[F]ederal crimes are defined by statute rather than by common law." Some lawyers and judges may be able to discern how Congress intended the statute to apply. But §848 does not provide the kind of notice that will enable ordinary people like the Johnson brothers to understand what conduct it prohibits.

Even if the Court were to find that the CCE statute does give fair notice as to some narrow category of conduct such as the term organizer, the statute in all cases fails adequately to restrain the discretion of judges, federal prosecutors or law enforcement.

The United States Supreme Court said, "Suppose a person who commits an unjustified homicide is prosecuted under a statute that says, 'It is a crime to do wrong.' The person surely had fair warning before he acted that his murderous conduct was 'wrong' and thus fell within the scope of the statute. Nevertheless, the statute is vague on its face, not because it provides insufficient notice, but because it does not provide sufficient minimal standards to guide law enforcement officers."

The Johnson brothers are subject to a thirty-year pine-box prison term for allegedly "managing, organizing, and supervising" a "continuing enterprise" and acquiring a "substantial income or earnings." However, the law does not define with particularity the role of a *manager, organizer, or supervisor*, or the actual activities that define the *"enterprise"*. The law does not define the duties associated with or required by the manager, organizer, or supervisor to be performed for the enterprise. The law does not define the meaning of *substantial income* or the proof required to prove the substantial income or earnings.

Yes, the statute says a person must generate $10 million in a twelve-month period. However, the law does not define the calculation method to prove the $10 million standard; it fails to state what gross receipts or financials the law considers to satisfy this element of CCE. The law does not establish when the enterprise starts or the definition of "continuing". It does not state the statute of limitations.

The brothers had intervals of several years between the alleged acts committed that do not support a finding of a "continuing criminal enterprise". The monies gathered are not proven to be directly associated with either brother, and even if some money was traceable, due to misconduct in collection reporting, then witnesses would be subject to giving perjured testimony or subject to impeachment. The government's case would be faced with the inability to prove beyond a reasonable doubt all of the elements of CCE and the underlying felony of money laundering.

If this case is any indication of the power of government and the fairness and integrity of the criminal justice system, then we are compelled to surmise that the government can guess at revenues of $10 million in gross receipts during any 12-month period for the manufacturer of a substance; they can guess at who is a principal, administrator, organizer, or leader, and the burden of persuasion shifts, forcing defendants to prove their innocence by a reasonable doubt. The U.S. Supreme Court has said that no one may be required at peril of life, liberty, or property to speculate as to the meaning of a penal law. Everyone is entitled to know what the government commands or forbids.

Attorney Communications and Inadequate Representations

Attorney Salmon had a conflict of interest because he continued to represent the interest of other defendants, cooperating and non-cooperating, apparently unbeknownst to Solomon.

When Solomon did not hear from Mr. Salmon, it appears from the record that Mr. Bill Fast became his attorney. Then his brother, Mr. Paul Fast, a family law attorney, conducted the plea hearing. Solomon did not have prior knowledge or notice of the new attorney or the plea. Mr. Fast had never presented the plea before the scheduled hearing. Solomon continued to profess his innocence of the charges and questioned the existence of evidence.

Neither Mr. B. Fast nor Mr. P. Fast filed any motions, as alleged. Mr. Fast claimed that he had verified the money judgment, filed for Speedy Trial, sought bond and release, deposed witnesses both cooperating and non-cooperating, sought dismissal of the indictment, challenged the CCE, and that he had verified Solomon's voice on the wiretaps. There exists no evidence in the court file of any of these activities. Finally, court-appointed public defender Kaplan Manner was Cali's appellate attorney. Manner never came to visit Solomon while he remained in Michigan and would not respond to his calls or letters about his case.

Conversely, if the attorneys had in fact deposed witnesses, then the Johnson brothers could have had the information needed to discredit their jury testimony and subject them to impeachment. Furthermore, if the attorneys had in fact challenged the indictment or the CCE statute as alleged as vague and ambiguous, David and Solomon could have proved that the law was unenforceable as applied and on its face and declared as void for vagueness. If the attorneys had engaged in reciprocal discovery, like they alleged, then the outcome would have been to separate the case between the brothers, because they had not spoken or interacted directly or indirectly in several years prior to the indictments. This information is confirmed by recorded statements and recordings of the federal agents who were on the case.

If the attorneys had moved the court for a pre-trial hearing on the issue of forfeiture, the Johnson brothers could have hired an attorney of choice. If the attorneys had moved the Court for a hearing to substantiate the alleged money judgment as alleged, then a hearing would have proven that neither brother conducted any "enterprise" or any business venture that supported income, proceeds, or revenue to verify or justify the $270 million money judgment.

Neither Fast nor Manner addressed the issue of the Motion to Withdraw the Guilty Plea, because the Johnson brothers did not knowingly and intelligently enter their pleas. The lawyers did not file the Motion to Dismiss the Indictment Due to Gross Government Misconduct based on altered, fabricated, stolen, or missing money from the vehicles, homes, and personal property. Further, no Motion to Identify the Confidential Informants had been filed. These are just a few of the injustices experienced by David and Solomon, which violated their Constitutional rights to effective assistance of counsel. Both brothers have held that they are innocent of the crimes accused in the indictment. Surely, if they knew their lawyers lied to them and that the record is devoid of the evidence alleged against them, they would not have entered a plea.

Rule 11 or Sentencing Hearing

When faced with ineffective assistance of counsel, it is impossible for a defendant to knowingly abandon a right or privilege whose existence he does not truly understand exists. If a defendant does not know he is a victim of ineffective assistance of counsel, then a Rule 11 colloquy does not assist the defendant in his understanding of whether he attained effective legal representation. For example, the transcript of the Rule 11 hearing shows that the Court never asked whether David or Solomon understood effective versus ineffective assistance of counsel, whether they understood reasonable diligence in legal representation, or whether they understood the actual work expected of attorneys in CCE and money laundering cases and against those measures if they deemed their plea as the acceptable alternative to trial.

A waiver is the "intentional relinquishment or abandonment of a known right or privilege." Although rights may be waived, courts "indulge every reasonable presumption against waiver of fundamental constitutional rights." To be valid, waivers must be knowing, intelligent, and voluntary. These rights can, of course, be waived. An examination of whether a person is "competent" is not the same as an examination of whether they are knowledgeable about the law and their Constitutional rights or the rights they waived.

The Rule 11 and Sentencing Hearing failed to secure from either David or Solomon whether they knew their lawyers were not effective and zealous during their representation, and whether, but for this knowledge, they would have entered a plea. The sentencing record lacks evidence to refute their contention that they knew their case could have successfully prevailed before trial or whether they knew that since their attorneys were not diligent in their representation, they could have gone to trial. Alternatively, the Johnson brothers did not know they did not have to enter a plea of guilty to the indicted offenses.

The record in their case establishes that the Court did not establish that they could consult with counsel and obtain a complete review of the sentencing guidelines. A waiver of an important constitutional or statutory right must be knowing and voluntary to be valid; therefore, prosecutors should ensure that the record reflects that the defendant knowingly and voluntarily waived his or her right to appeal the sentence. There is no evidence that the brothers knowingly waived their right to appeal their plea under the sentencing guidelines provision.

Appeal

Did they file an appeal or seek to withdraw their pleas? Yes. However, they filed for appeals on different grounds. It appears they were unaware that they were victims of ineffective assistance of counsel on these grounds. When Solomon filed his appeal, his court-appointed defense attorney filed an Anders brief stating his appeal was frivolous. His lawyer did not raise all possible legal issues for appeal, he did not identify any of these issues, and the record supports reason for appellate review and existence of errors; therefore, in light of these issues, it is clear that his court-appointed attorney engaged in ineffective assistance of counsel.

The Supreme Court has set a high standard for determining what constitutes a satisfactory Anders brief; however, it appears that Manner never (emphasis added) submitted his brief to Solomon to review before filing it with the Court of Appeals. Moreover, he never considered the written communications from Solomon to his attention about withdrawal of the plea on other grounds or concerns about representation, or his request to furnish a copy of his case file. David and Solomon are businessmen; they are not attorneys or men of legal minds.

Possible Solutions

Bear in mind that the brothers can challenge their pleas and forfeitures because their 30-year mandatory minimum sentences, unsubstantiated $270,000,000 money judgment, and forfeiture of millions of dollars in real and personal property violate the Fourth, Fifth, Sixth, Eighth (Excessive Fine Clause and Cruel and Unusual Punishment), and Fourteenth Amendments of the U.S. Constitution. Solomon's plea bargaining sentence also violates the Sixth Amendment Guarantee of effective assistance of counsel, because his counselor, Mr. Daniels, failed to disclose that he was facing death as a result of cancer and that he was using heavy medication, which impaired his quality of representation.

What this means is that if afforded an opportunity to file a motion to vacate, set aside or correct a sentence, provided under 28 U.S.C. § 2255, the brothers will be able to show the Court that their acceptance of their plea and their convictions are not proper and that the violations of their constitutional rights to effective assistance of counsel adversely affect their substantial rights of fairness, integrity, or public reputation of the proceedings and that they are entitled to relief. During the 1990s, the mandatory minimum sentence would have been a 10-year punishment for the crimes they were accused of in 2005.

Disparate impact, discriminatory enforcement of laws and punishment, and the prejudicial abuse of discretion exist against minorities subject to drug laws sentencing. Surely, members of Heaven's Angels, Brotherhood, Dixie Town, and others are the subject of pine box sentences, but CCE adversely impacts minority defendants. R.I.C.O. laws are generally applied against crimes committed by white males, and their sentences are less. Money laundering is the underlying felony under the Johnson brothers' CCE conviction. Money laundering is also the underlying offense under R.I.C.O. Plea bargaining could have caused the brothers to be sentenced to ten years under R.I.C.O.

Twelve

The Journey Begins

"Deserves it! I daresay he does. Many that live deserve death. And some that die deserve life. Can you give it to them? Then do not be too eager to deal out death in judgement. For even the very wise cannot see all ends."
J.R.R. Tolkien, *The Fellowship of the Ring*

On the morning of November 8, 2007, David and Solomon Johnson awoke to learn that they were scheduled for court. They thought the scheduled hearing was to consider their motion for bail. The Johnson brothers had been incarcerated since 2005. Their lawyers received almost two million dollars to pay a cash bond, but the brothers sat behind bars from 2005 through 2007. They reluctantly entered pleas of guilty. David met very briefly with his attorney, who told him he would face life imprisonment or could face the death penalty if he did not accept the plea. Solomon met his new lawyer on the morning of the plea hearing, and he also reluctantly entered a plea of guilty based on the same misrepresentation. At the time, neither David nor Solomon knew they were victims of ineffective assistance of counsel. After they entered their pleas, the judge scheduled the sentencing hearing for September 2008.

It is September 12, 2008, and The Journey Begins. Imagine hearing, "Mr. Johnson, I hereby sentence you to 30 years to serve in the United States penitentiary." David looked back in the courtroom to see the prosecutor laughing at his mother as she cried before the Court. For the first time, he saw her pain. She had witnessed the loss of two sons and the father of her children. It was more than she could bear. Meanwhile, Solomon stood before the Court and received his sentence.

Their mother was not a well-versed or educated woman. She did not understand the criminal justice system. She had no idea how to challenge what had happened to her family. They did not have any assets to defend against the government; the system is designed that way. It is designed to charge people with a crime, seize their assets, and prevent them from defending against the accusations.

The Journey Begins with three hots and a cot. From mansions to a block shared with two to three men. From eating at the finest restaurants and having chefs prepare your food to eating prison food. The Journey Begins from having privacy to showering and using the restroom in the presence of others. From visiting people, places, and things to being told when someone can visit you. The thirty-year journey begins.

The Journey Begins from calling anyone at any time to being told when you can call. From having all the clothes, money, jewelry, and personal items you desire to wearing a prison uniform and waiting for people to put money on your books for commissary. No more family or game nights. Surely, the Johnson brothers will possibly never dance or play a hand of cards again. The Journey Begins from having your own gym to less than an hour of recreation time. From being able to provide for your family and attend to their needs to now needing someone to attend to your needs. The Journey Begins from being there to assist your parents when they are sick and watching your children grow up to learning that your parents are very ill and not being at their side. The thirty-year journey begins.

During the first year of their 30-year bit, David and Solomon sat silently while people shared their war stories, and most of the stories were lies, blatant lies. People had dramatized their story in a way that caused more harm than good. Like rough riders who slip and fall, during the first year the Johnson brothers went on a bus ride. Early morning wake-up call; 4-piece and get on the bus to be transported like cattle. Housed or in the bing in Georgia, Pennsylvania, California, Louisiana, and Florida. The feds continuously transferred them to different prisons to break down any influence they thought they had in the system. All of their family, friends, and colleagues were incarcerated and serving five to thirty years. No one could investigate their cases. The journey continues.

By the fifth year of incarceration, David and Solomon continued to be subject to the bus rides. No one available to investigate their cases, and as people were back on deck and released from prison, due to no contact provisions, they were unable to get information about pleas, assets, or representation. Most of the people they knew did not possess legal minds. The Bureau of Prisons does not grant access to Pacers or court files. The journey continues, and it has been ten years since the Johnson brothers have been buried in the belly of the beast.

Thirteen

Understanding the Journey

**"Justice will not be served until those who are unaffected
are as outraged as those who are."
Benjamin Franklin**

Law and order are essential in any modern society. Urban corridors in America epitomize segregation, poverty, drugs, and despair. These elements converge on youth, and they question their future. The police mobilize and are militarized to fight the war on drugs. The inner city youth become prisoners and enemies of war. Inner cities across America are plagued by C.R.A.P. (**Corruption, Racism, Abuse, & Politics**). To escape the inner city blues, one must run away, move up, or move out. Understanding the journey means recognizing the forces that draw people to crime.

The Johnson brothers had the audacity to discern a better way of life that offered lucrative opportunities. If true, hundreds of independent contractors obtained employment. However, throughout history the American Dream is premised upon supply and demand and commodity and human capital. From slavery to present day, freedom and opportunity are the set of ideals that define the American Dream. The journey continues.

What is the difference between David and Solomon Johnson and CEOs of the world's leading pharmaceutical companies? Taxation and a demand for market share.

One of the most influential and wealthiest families in America history engaged in smuggling illegal drugs or alcohol. The family violated criminal laws and raised a future president, a senator, and an Attorney General of the United States. Children are not destined to start or finish their parents' journey, and many would rather not do so. The Johnson brothers journeyed through unchartered waters, forging alliances, acquiring wealth, possessing celebrity status, and becoming successful businessmen. Most interesting about their journey is that ten years after their arrest and conviction, they remain a topic of discussion. Understanding the journey means recognizing institutional racism and being willing to stand against it.

The journey is not for studio gangsters who cannot live or interpret this life absent living this life. The lore of convincing young children to sell drugs and embrace material possessions through music is profitable, but the journey of the people who travel the road is deadly. American prisons are full of men like the Johnson brothers who could have reigned over Fortune 500 companies, but instead are living in bondage. Understand the journey.

Urban legend; the odyssey of two of America's most wanted and their family transcends drugs, music, money, and material possessions. Their journey gives proponents and opponents of the war on drugs a lesson to learn. To the press, the Johnson brothers were hard core men who kept their mind on their riches. The press and public labeled these men as those who had a taste for Louis Roederer Cristal champagne and Perrier Jouet Rosé, traveled in style in Rolls-Royce Phantoms, Lamborghinis Murcielago, and Aston Martins Vanquish, and spent hundreds of thousands of dollars on entertainment. The journey continues.

To their friends and family, the Johnson brothers were God fearing, loving providers and men of fortitude. To law enforcement, prosecutors, and judges, the Johnson men were two of America's most wanted who deserve to die beyond the wall for violating criminal laws, no matter how vague, ambiguous, and arbitrarily or discriminatorily enforced. Understanding the journey means acknowledging the existence of injustice and working toward criminal justice reform.

After ten years of serving their 30-year pine box sentence for alleged violations of money laundering, David and Solomon continue to face their adversity with their heads held high. The Johnson brothers continue to value, embrace, and honor their principles of loyalty, integrity, honesty, dignity, and death before dishonor. Surely, David and Solomon could have cooperated with the federal authorities and lied on people; instead, they recognized the error of their ways. Understanding the journey means being accountable and responsible for past misjudgments.

The Johnson brothers are innocent as accused in the indictments and are victims of ineffective assistance of counsel. It goes without saying that parents want more for their children than they acquired for themselves. Surely, David and Solomon had an opportunity to make other life choices; however, should Americans ignore a failed criminal justice system, ineffective assistance of counsel, and a total and reckless disregard of the U.S. Constitution and Bill of

Rights? The audacity to think big should not end in a 30-year life sentence. The war on drugs continues ten years after they began serving their pine box sentence. Is America any safer? Is America a drug-free society? America's shame.

Compare and contrast the effects of illicit drugs to prescription drugs, and according to research conducted by a U.S. government agency, "Every day, 44 people in the United States die from overdose from prescription painkillers, and many more become addicted...the United States is in the midst of a prescription painkiller overdose epidemic. Since 1999, the amount of prescription painkillers prescribed and sold in the U.S. has nearly quadrupled, yet there has not been an overall change in the amount of pain that Americans report. Overprescribing leads to more abuse and more overdose deaths." Is the world any safer with David and Solomon incarcerated under a 30-year prison term? Understanding the journey means being willing to repeal, abolish, or amend laws.

The Bureau of Prisons housed David in a maximum security prison located in the state of Colorado. An argument for the legalization of marijuana has won the support of Colorado voters. BOP houses inmates charged with the illegal drug trafficking of marijuana. Controlled substances used in prescription drugs possess the exact same ingredients used by drug dealers who sell marijuana, cocaine, heroin, and meth.

The war on drugs is controlled by three entities: governments who use illegal drug proceeds to finance unnecessary wars and weapons of mass destruction in other countries; the pharmaceutical companies who use drugs for curative, preventive health, but also know people will become addicted to prescription drugs; and cartels who manage the distribution of illicit drugs for personal reasons to combat their realities of dealing with poverty, and who furnish drugs to people who cannot afford prescription drugs and the cost associated with getting medical and mental health services. At some point, all three of these entities share greed as their common goal.

The cartels are the only ones who suffer the greatest consequences of their actions, even where evidence demonstrates that the abuse of prescription drugs leads to unaccountable deaths and destruction in families and communities. The war on drugs is an inequitable feat. Our nation's Founding Fathers never envisioned when they ratified the 4th, 5th, 6th, 8th and 14th Amendments to the United States Constitution that the War on Drugs would mean citizens would be victims of blatant infringements. America's shame.

The Founding Fathers never envisioned that law enforcement, prosecutors, and judges would forge an alliance. The Founding Fathers never envisioned that Americans would be guilty until proven innocent and that the government would deny the fundamental rights guaranteed under the Constitution to ensure effective assistance of counsel, no matter the charge. Confidential informants, secret grand juries, sealed indictments, and forfeitures are deficiencies in the criminal justice system. The inability to hire an attorney of choice, prisoner denial of records and access to court documents, conflicted judges, and a system that defines Americans by past judgments – once a felon, always a felon - are deficiencies in the criminal justice system. Understanding the journey.

The desire to live the American Dream drives people to the lure of money, homes, and vehicles. For many, this is the definition of success. For others, the American Nightmare is a 30-year mortgage, a 25-year student loan repayment plan, and unemployment or the inability to obtain employment in a field of learning. The use of public housing, education, healthcare, transportation, and public legal defense are the only options most Americans are able to attain, in spite of all their efforts. Respectfully, anything having the word 'public' is generally tragic and inadequate. Understanding the journey means acknowledging inequities.

The American Dream is a fallacy. The Dream is a trick to lure people to survive by any means necessary. The reality for families like the Johnsons is that life's bare essentials (food, water, and shelter) drive some people to engage in illegal acts to survive, and its ultimate impact is the poverty-to-prison pipeline.

For most Americans, to live the American Dream means to make fast food or make fast money; the working poor have jobs that keep them **just over broke**. Incarcerating men and women under pine box sentences has not and will never resolve the war on drugs. Understanding the journey means acknowledging that we have created circumstances that make people commit crimes to survive.

America has a **1-Strike criminal justice system**, because upon arrest, whether wrongfully accused or not, an offender is denied **housing, health care, educational opportunities, and employment (H.E.M.S). They are incapable of maintaining and supporting** themselves. The impact upon the H.E.M.S. means a life of crime is inevitable. Families of persons serving mandatory minimums are unable to survive with parents or children incarcerated.

Children of incarcerated parents are more likely to be juvenile delinquents, drop out of school, or be victims of the school-to-prison pipeline or the prostitution and sexual abuse-to-prison pipeline. Children of incarcerated parents are more likely to be unwed and teenage, single parents, live in poverty, and become part of the poverty-to-prison pipeline. All of these variables continue the cycle of drug use, a demand for 'illegal' drugs, and drug dealing. Conversely, the demand for prescription drugs, meth, cocaine and laced cannabis is a growing demand among white, middle class, suburban Americans. Will every American soon become a prisoner of the war on drugs or the drug war?

Former presidential candidate Shirley Chisholm said:

> *"It is not heroin or cocaine that makes one an addict, it is the need to escape from a harsh reality. There are more television addicts, more baseball and football addicts, more movie addicts, and certainly more alcohol addicts in this country than there are narcotics addicts."*

It has been 44 years since the United States waged its war on drugs. America lost its so-called War on Drugs because it never fought or won the battles against addiction and mental health, poverty and inequitable distribution of wealth, institutionalized racism and discrimination, and its tragic public system - failed public system - of schools, housing, and healthcare. America's shame. Are you your brother's keeper?

In America, prison is the only guarantee of three
meals, a warm bed, electricity, running water,
and heat from the coldness of this world.
With a 30-year pine box sentence,
the Johnson brothers are guaranteed no eviction.

EPILOGUE

The doors to America's criminal justice system are revolving not re-entry.
Sherri Jefferson

Social Issues and the Human Cost of the War on Drugs

According to the U.S. Substance Abuse and Mental Health Service (SAMHSA) Department, drug use in America includes opioids, tobacco, and alcohol; therefore, when people consider data and research about drug use and abuse in America, it includes two legalized 'drugs' of tobacco and alcohol.

America invested in citizens, communities, and economic development, and citizens gave back by becoming productive contributors to society. In the late 1960s and early 70s, major cities within the United States were ravaged by the heroin epidemic. Most of the addicts were teenagers and young adults. Many minorities returned home from fighting the Vietnam War and were addicts.

During the 1960s and 1970s, some social programs helped families in need. To address alcohol and narcotics addiction, states initiated treatment programs. America treated alcoholism as a disease and created community-based treatment programs for counseling. The implementation of programs included provisions to address poverty and criminal justice diversion. President Johnson appointed the first National Advisory Committee on Alcoholism and became the first president to address the country about alcoholism.

The so-called War on Drugs has caused some legislators, advocates, and communities to demand longer prison terms in lieu of prevention or intervention measures. The 1970 Congress passed the "Comprehensive Alcohol Abuse and Alcoholism Prevention Treatment and Rehabilitation Act", known as the Hughes Act; however, the Nixon administration invested little in the fight against alcohol addiction.

Nixon called drug abuse "public enemy number one" in a 1971 speech; he emphasized treatment at first and then used his administration's clout to push for the criminalization of drug users, particularly heroin addicts. The Drug Abuse Treatment Act of 1972 created the Special Action Office for Drug Abuse Prevention but allotted very few resources for prevention against heroin addicts. By 1973, the United States had created a Drug Enforcement Agency (DEA).

To combat drugs, alcoholism, and poverty, the Johnson Administration created social programs. The Nixon and Ford Administrations enhanced some social programs that included the Head Start program. These programs doubled the chances of gainful employment later in life. Employment and educational training programs helped underserved communities and people incarcerated. The federally funded lunch and dinner programs aided families in need. The hiring of first-time offenders and not reporting juvenile offenses enabled prior offenders a fresh start, and summer employment programs helped teenagers learn a trade and work. The summer programs also reduced crime. Some social reform programs worked, and others did not, like the destruction of public housing projects and forcing people to move into subsidized housing in "middle class" neighborhoods.

Today, instead of developing alternatives to address drug addiction, employment opportunities, and educational services, we would rather arrest, charge, convict, and incarcerate. Enacting legislation to combat drug dealing is necessary, but as necessary is the enactment of legislation that mandates drug, substance abuse, and mental health treatment. We need early intervention and prevention programs at K-12; we need prison rehabilitation programs that would require the completion of high school diplomas or GEDs, and vocational training or college education. This would give an opportunity for individuals to re-enter society. Currently, we stigmatize offenders, but if we offered a fresh start, akin to bankruptcy laws and credit reporting laws, by enacting a **Fair Criminal Records Reporting Act** that would delete criminal histories after a period of time, then people would not be required to report their arrests for non-violent and some other violent offenses that are examined on a case-by-case basis.

The Act could authorize the removal and deletion of criminal histories after two years for a misdemeanor, and seven years from the date of sentence completion for non-violent and some other felonies. A pardon, a commuted sentence, the vacating of a conviction, and restricting and expunging records **do not** provide the same safeguards and guarantees of record deletion, because the criminal histories are available to local, state, and federal authorities, as well as certain members of the public sector, including law enforcement departments, court clerks and jail records. Reporting is required for financial aid, college admission, and employment. Even with a *ban-the-box* provision, criminal background checks are performed at the time of application, and criminal histories are present in the background check. Reporting is also required for professional boards like nursing, even where an expungement is granted. Moreover, a person arrested or convicted of a crime, must honestly answer to their past misjudgments because the background check will also reveal it. In America, a person can incur a million dollars in debt, file bankruptcy and within two years purchase a new home or vehicle. Within seven to ten years, their bankruptcy is removed and deleted from their credit report and all public and private agencies. They never have to report their filings. In America, a 17-year old can illegally enter an automobile or engage in theft and will be required to report these incidents until the day of his death so long as he is seeking a H.E.M.S. of housing, education, employment, maintenance or support. He needs a Fair Chance not just a second chance with barriers of forgiveness.

Best said, imagine a spouse who cheats on their mate during marriage. Now imagine that the spouse seeks a second chance at restoring the marriage, but the mate always reminds the spouse of their past discretions and misjudgments. Is that a second chance or a fair chance at reconciliation? There is a difference.

A hindrance to successful reconciliation of past misjudgments for former offenders is that the privatization of the prison industrial complex infringes on these options because it is not cost-effective to prevent people from reoffending. Recidivism is the agenda in the profit-sharing business of prisons. Mass incarceration is profitable in America because the private companies who own and manage prisons trade on the stock market. Supervising inmates on probation is also profitable, and the abusive practices of this industry leads to peonage. Cost includes fees for supervision, surcharges, court fines, drug testing, etc.

Human Investment

Today, homelessness, human trafficking, mental health, dysfunctional families, the school-to-prison pipeline, and failed public housing and education have resulted in a drug dependent society. Longer prison terms and no treatment adversely impact society. The government forgets that children and addicts are the victims of long prison terms. Taxpayers have invested $14.2 billion in the War on Drugs for correctional expenditures. Victims of criminal records, long prison terms, and collateral consequences associated with arrest and conviction prevent America from successfully competing in a global society.

The criminal justice system itself is a threat to national security, because future scientists, technologists, engineers, and mathematicians are subject to the penal system or persons are not capable to serve in the armed forces because of criminal records. Victims of the so-called War on Drugs, African American children represent less than 25% of the general school-aged population in the United States; however, in most jurisdictions in this country, they represent more than 60% of the children subject to arrest, conviction, and incarceration for school-related offenses. According to the FBI, recent data shows that African American girls represent 59.5% of persons arrested under the age of 18 for prostitution. These children are the victims of human trafficking and child sexual slavery. The criminalization of their victimization sends them to the jailhouse, as opposed to a safe house.

The Nixon, Reagan, and Clinton Administrations were pro-war on drugs. Their administrations passed some of the harshest laws and prison terms. New York legislator Charles Rangel pushed for tough drug laws that ultimately became known as the disparity between crack and cocaine sentencing. Minorities are victims of the disparate impact. Since the passage of SB 1789 in August 2010, the Obama Administration has not released any offenders subject to disparity in sentencing for crack v. cocaine offenses, and respectfully, the administration has been all-but silent on the issue of drug abuse in America.

President Obama's Administration has pushed legislation to address some reform, which includes an Executive Order to *ban-the-box* that seeks information about conviction at the time of application. But, as previously discussed that does not give an ex-offender a second chance because he has to continue to disclose his past misjudgments at some point prior to hiring. President Obama Administration has also provided funding for some programs to assist juveniles with re-entry, but has not addressed the collateral consequences associated with arrest and/or conviction or the dismantling of the school-to-prison pipeline. The administration has not addressed the disparity and arbitrary enforcement of drug laws in America that have led to an explosive prison population.

A **Fair Criminal Records Reporting Act** is the only way to ensure that criminal records do not prevent people from having a fair chance at re-entry in America. Americans need more than a second chance; they need a fair chance. In fact, we know that most laws that lead to arrest are void for vagueness and unconstitutional. We know that most people of color and the poor are victims of unnecessary arrest that led to collateral consequences even after dismissal as well as arbitrary and discriminatory enforcement of laws. America's shame.

The author hopes this publication sheds light on the unresolved issues associated with mandatory minimums, 3-Strikes legislation, and pine box sentences. Its awareness of the controversy of the war on drugs will hopefully engender a debate to create an international and national call to action on the issue. We can no longer talk about the issue, we must enact new laws and develop programs and services for defendants and victims of drug offenses. We cannot offer college education and Pell grants to inmates and deny Pell grants and college admission to persons with criminal records under the 'Gainful Employment' standards.

The unfairness or blatant disregard for the freedoms guaranteed in the U.S. Constitution and Bill of Rights is the legacy of the war on drugs. The use of militarized police and violation of the 4th, 5th, 6th, 8th and Fourteenth Amendments are the legacy of the War on Drugs, due to unauthorized searches and seizures, violations of the rights against self-incrimination, ineffective assistance of counsel through some public funding legal defense programs, or their inability to finance a legal defense against the government. The inability to review discovery, provide expert testimony, secure witnesses, or conduct fair, effective, and proper investigations and violating the Excessive Bail Clause are some of the disregards for the freedoms guaranteed under the Constitution.

The privatization of the prison industrial and probationary system includes the for-profit business of bail, the need to pay to upwards of $3.00 per minute for a collect and or direct telephone call and the enormous fees associated with this service, which includes forcing people to switch telephone carriers. The for-profit business includes forfeiture of assets, fines, fees, surcharges, drug and alcohol testing and other fees. In addition, it is unconscionable that a person cannot notify family of an arrest and detention unless they have money on their books, and in order to get money on their books they have to be able to make a call. Commissary for basic necessities like pens, paper, stamps, undergarments, socks, etc. is highway robbery. It is unconscionable that families must pay upwards of $5.00 for a pair of undergarments. This system makes reform almost impossible. Families should be able to make their own purchases from their own stores of choice. We must dismantle the for-profit to prison pipeline.

Do mandatory minimums and longer prison terms prevent drug trafficking? No, is the definitive answer. The United States Department of Justice and Congress have been unable to definitively prove that harsher penal laws and their get tough on crime approach have changed the outcome of crime or drug trafficking. On the other hand, tough on crime proponents have criticized legislators, citing that the penal laws are not enforced and the sentences are not tough enough in comparison to the harm created by drug use. On June 26, 2015, the U.S. Supreme Court struck down part of the 3-Strikes provision under the Armed Career Criminal Act, defining what crimes make a defendant eligible for a longer prison term as too vague and unconstitutional. Intentional, willful, wanton, malicious, and knowingly engaging in arbitrary and discriminatory enforcement of laws demonstrates the great lengths the government has taken to punish people for drug offenses.

BEYOND THE BOOK: Reader's Circle

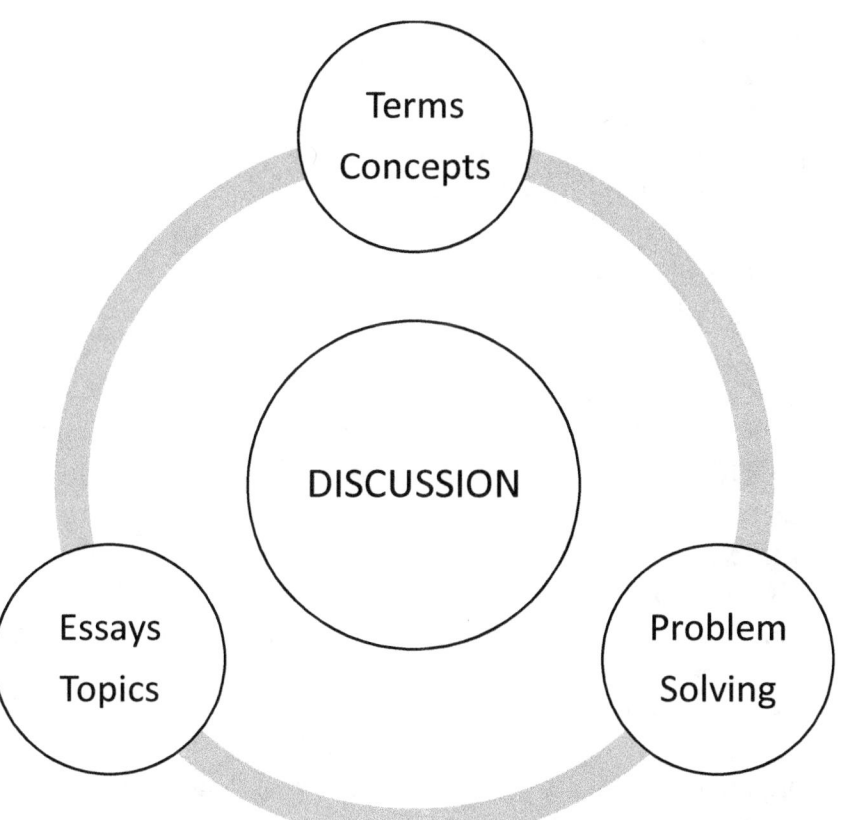

Terms Concepts

DISCUSSION

Essays Topics

Problem Solving

IMPORTANT TERMS AND CONCEPTS

1. Supply and demand
2. Capital
3. Economics
4. Monopoly
5. Fair distribution of income
6. Income
7. Entrepreneur
8. Recidivism
9. Profit Sharing
10. Competition
11. FBI
12. DEA
13. CIA
14. HIDTA
15. Trafficking
16. Dealer
17. Cartel
18. Defendant
19. Law
20. Dichotomy
21. Indictment
22. Plea
23. Verdict
24. Sentence
25. Grand Jury
26. Legislator
27. Rockefeller Drug Laws
28. Mandatory minimums
29. RICO

30. CCE
31. 3-Strikes
32. Felon
33. Felony
34. Misdemeanor
35. Violent Crime Control and Law Enforcement Act
36. Armed Career Criminal Act
37. Taxation
38. Partnership
39. Corporation
40. Independent Contractor
41. Civil Rights Act
42. Voting Rights Act
43. Exposition
44. Execrable
45. Counterproductive
46. Reform
47. Criminal justice
48. Urbanology
49. Hoodology
50. Gentrification
51. Social reform
52. Social programs
53. Immigration
54. Migration
55. Constitutional
56. Void for Vagueness
57. Ambiguous
58. Unconstitutional
59. Discrimination
60. Arbitrary
61. Privatization of Prison Industrial Complex
62. Prosecutor
63. Forfeiture

64. Assets
65. Welfare recipients
66. Aid to Families with dependent children
67. Domestic violence
68. Autonomy
69. Operating leverage
70. Anti-Trust
71. Vicarious Liability

DISCUSSION TOPICS

1. Modern Day Slavery and Human Trafficking
2. The War on Drugs and what it means to you
3. Drug Addiction and Mental Health
4. Corruption, Racism, Abuse and Politics (CRAP)
5. How can the 6Ps (parents, pastors, principals, police, prosecutors and police) help to prevent crime in America?
6. Difference, if any, between drug use among the Middle Class and the Inner City
7. How the government handled crack addiction versus meth and prescription pill use
8. Genocide in Rwanda
9. Advocate for a Fair Criminal Records Reporting Act that would delete non-violent criminal records after a period – as credit reports delete histories. Re-entry and second chance program 'Project Fresh Start'.
10. Shirley Chisholm and Hillary Clinton
11. HIV/AIDS in America
12. How important are Historically Black Colleges and Universities in the new millennium?
13. Should we legalize cocaine in America?
14. Should we treat everyone equally under the law?
15. What is justice?
16. What criminal sentence do you think is fair for the Johnson brothers, and why?

ESSAY TOPICS

1. Social Reform vs. Social Programs
2. Criminal Justice Reform
3. How can the 6Ps (parents, pastors, principal, police, prosecutors and police) help to prevent or reduce crime in America?
4. Should we legalize cocaine in America?
5. Will the legalization of drugs be the action necessary to winning the war on drugs?
6. Explain the challenges and crises in the war on drugs in relation to America
7. What are the political challenges facing the war on drugs?
8. What are the social challenges to winning the war on drugs?
9. What are the economic challenges facing the war on drugs?
10. What changes must America make to win the war on drugs?
11. Explain the privatization of the prison industrial complex. Does for-profit prison prevent criminal justice reform?
12. Corruption, Racism, Abuse and Politics (CRAP)
13. Discuss the women's suffrage movement and the struggles of African American women in America
14. Are minorities likely to be sentenced under CCE and mandatory minimum sentences?
15. Is the criminal justice system color blind or blinded by color?
16. If you were the president, what would your drug

prevention and control plan be for America?

17. Compare and contrast Black youth from the 1960s to African American youth of today
18. Has America lost the war on drugs?
19. Choose a decade and write about drug use, drug laws, and the war on drugs
20. Is criminalizing drug use the best way to solve addiction?
21. What happened to the U.S. automotive industry giants?
22. What happened to the Bell Telecommunication companies in the 1980s?
23. Advocate for a Fair Criminal Records Reporting Act that would delete non-violent criminal records after a period – as credit reports delete histories. Re-entry and second chance program 'Project Fresh Start'.
24. How has the North American Free Trade Agreement influenced the American economy?
25. Compare the leaders of the 1960s to the leaders of today
26. If Martin Luther King, Jr., Malcolm X, and President Kennedy were alive today, what would be their speaking platform or agenda for change?
27. Compare and contrast two poems, choosing one from Langston Hughes, James Baldwin, Nikki Giovanni, and Maya Angelou
28. Explain the post-war decline in marriage in America
29. Identify the struggles of Black women in America in the 1960s and today
30. Discuss the heroin epidemic and servicemen returning from the Vietnam War
31. Discuss 'white flight' and how it influences diversity and the economics of the community
32. Discuss Martha Griffith and the Equal Rights

Amendment
33. Are drugs laws in America discriminatory (discuss the Harrison Act, Marijuana Tax and other laws?)
34. What effect has gangsta rap had on America?
35. How have abortions and the Roe v. Wade decision impacted America?
36. Is the administration of laws important?
37. Should we treat everyone equally under the law?
38. What is justice?
39. Do longer prison terms prevent crime?
40. How do longer prison terms impact society?
41. What criminal sentence do you think is fair for the Johnson brothers, and why?

QUESTIONS FOR THOUGHT TO STIMULATE CONVERSATION AND ADVOCACY

1. Discuss drugs and America's involvement in the Russian–Soviet and Afghan war
2. Discuss whether the CIA funded crack cocaine in Black communities in the 1980s
3. What is Black studies, and is it necessary in America?
4. Define the student movement of the 1960s and compare to the #Blacklivesmatter movement and use of social media today
5. What are the political, social, and economic concerns for youth in America?
6. What is multiculturalism?
7. Does racism exist? Explain and give examples
8. Do we need mandatory minimum prison terms, or should judges be able to freely sentence?
9. What is the difference between the presidential campaigns or agendas of Shirley Chisholm (1972), Jesse Jackson (1984), and Barack Obama (2008 and 2012)?
10. What is racism?
11. What is the ghetto, or the 'hood?
12. What solution do you propose to end poverty?
13. What is a political party, and what is politics?
14. Choose a decade and discuss some of the challenges and achievements of combating the so-called war on drugs
15. Has immigration influenced drug dealing, drug addiction, or the war on drugs in America?

16. Corruption, Racism, Abuse and Politics (CRAP)
17.
18. Which presidential administration best handled drug prevention and control in America?
19. What is the school-to-prison pipeline? How do we dismantle it?
20. What is the sexual abuse-to-prison pipeline? How do we end trafficking – modern day slavery - and the pipeline that leads to prison?
21. If you were the Johnson brothers, what investment would you have made in your community?
22. Does America's criminal justice system forgive?
23. What do you think about public housing, school, transportation, and public health care, and how can we improve these systems?
24. Did the welfare program destroy families in need by preventing fathers from remaining in the home as a requirement for government assistance?
25. What is the dichotomy of NWA and NWB?
26. How can the 6Ps (parents, pastors, principal, police, prosecutors and police) help to prevent or reduce crime in America?
27. Advocate for a Fair Criminal Records Reporting Act that would delete non-violent criminal records after a period – as credit reports delete histories. Re-entry and second chance program 'Project Fresh Start'.

PROBLEMS REQUIRING CALCULATION, GRAPHING AND SYNTHESIS

1. How much money has the United States spent on the war on drugs since 1971?
2. How much money does the United States (or your individual state) spend on housing an inmate versus to educate each student in schools?
3. How much money does it cost to incarcerate one person for 10 years in a federal or state prison?
4. Make a graph and show the number of people incarcerated in your state by race, gender, and age
5. What is a kilo?
6. What is a sack?
7. What is a money counter?
8. How many kilos must a person sell to make $10 million dollars in one year? How many kilos must they sell each month, and at what cost?
9. How much annual tax must a person pay to the IRS on gross revenues of $10 million?
10. What would you do with one million dollars, and why? Explain your spending habits and calculate.
11. Create a graph of the number of inmates incarcerated in your state by crime (show violent versus non-violent crimes).

ACTIVITIES

1. Project Stay in Touch (adopt a juvenile detention center, women's prison - send cards, letters of encouragement, etc.)
2. Start a support group at your school, church, or community for children of incarcerated parents
3. Mentor
4. Volunteer at established programs
5. Support community and faith-based prison ministry
6. Advocate against mandatory minimums, pine box sentences, and life without parole
7. Start a Project 6Ps in your home, school, church, or community
8. Advocate against the school-to-prison pipeline
9. Create petitions to bring awareness
10. Host family night or host game night
11. Host a family for food, fun, and fellowship
12. Create an awareness program for foster care and services
13. Become a foster parent or adopt a child
14. Advocate for video conferencing in prison and the reduction of the cost associated with calling and staying in touch with loved ones who are incarcerated
15. Advocate for reduction of cost of commissary items or for the ability to purchase items through vendors of choice for less money
16. Advocate against telecommunication Con companies who charge enormous fees for per minute telephone calls and for every person incarcerated to be able to have an email account (like CORRS system)

17.   Advocate for incarcerated persons to have access to online court records via PACER or another program

18.   Advocate for schools to remain open during summer breaks and holidays as a safe haven for families in need of child care services

19.   Advocate for summer employment, lunch and dinner programs during the school year and breakfast, lunch and dinner programs during the summer and for funding for arts and music programs

20.   Advocate for community centers to remain open

21.   Advocate for a Fair Criminal Records Reporting Act that would delete non-violent criminal records after a period – as credit reports delete histories. Re-entry and second chance program 'Project Fresh Start'.

WORKS CITED

1. Jones, Van. "Our Justice System is Broken" http://www.justicereformnow.org (2015)
2. NAACP. Criminal Justice Fact Sheet. http://www.naacp.org/pages/criminal-justice-fact-sheet (2015)
3. Study: 7.3 million in U.S. prison system in '07 http://www.cnn.com/2009/CRIME/03/02/record.prison.population/ (2009)
4. Carson, Ann E. BJS Statistician. "Prisoners in 2013" http://www.bjs.gov/content/pub/pdf/p13.pdf (2015)
5. Federal Bureau of Stats. "Inmate Race" https://www.bop.gov/about/statistics/statistics_inmate_race.jsp (September 26, 2015)
6. Sentencing Project. "Hispanic Prisoners in the United States" http://www.sentencingproject.org/doc/publications/inc_hispanicprisoners.pdf
7. Children and Families of the Incarcerated Fact Sheet. https://nrccfi.camden.rutgers.edu/files/nrccfi-fact-sheet-2014.pdf
8. Pew Research Center. "Hispanic Trends". http://www.pewhispanic.org (September 28. 2015)
9. "A Look at the 1940 Census". https://www.census.gov/newsroom/cspan/1940census/CSPAN_1940slides.pdf

10. Dan, Joseph. "Nearly 50 Million Abortions Have Been Performed in U.S. Since Roe V. Wade Decision Legalized Abortion" http://cnsnews.com/news/article/nearly-50-million-abortions-have-been-performed-us-roe-v-wade-decision-legalized

11. Evans, Laurie. "Abortion Surveillance --- United States, 2000" http://www.cdc.gov/mmwr/preview/mmwrhtml/ss5212a1.htm

12. Gray, Madison. "New York's Rockefeller Laws" http://content.time.com/time/nation/article/0,8599,1888864,00.html (April 02, 2009)

13. ""Three Strikes" Sentencing Laws". http://criminal.findlaw.com/criminal-procedure/three-strikes-sentencing-laws.html#sthash.LZ9vptNS.dpuf (2015)

14. White, Williams. "Significant Events in the History of Addiction Treatment and

15. Recovery in America" http://www.williamwhitepapers.com/pr/AddictionTreatment&RecoveryInAmerica.pdf (2015)

16. Eisenach, Jeffrey and Cowin, Andrew. "The Case Against More Funds for Drug Treatment" http://www.heritage.org/research/reports/1991/05/bg829-the-case-against-more-funds-for-drug-treatment (1991)

17. Id

18. Id

19. Mayor Giuliani Calls for End of Methadone Treatment in New York. http://ndsn.org/sepoct98/treat2.html

20. Drug War 40 Years Later. https://youtu.be/jtZaWLOSiWA CNN Drug War 40 Years Later

21. Jefferson, Sherri. "Dismantle the School to Prison Pipeline". https://attorneysherrijefferson.wordpress.com/2015/10/01/threat-to-national-security-it-is-necessary-to-dismantle-the-school-to-prison-pipeline-by-sherri-jefferson (2015)

22. Barbash, Jack. "Unions and Rights in the Space Age" http://www.dol.gov/dol/aboutdol/history/chapter6.htm

23. Meyer, Stephen. "The Degradation of Work Revisited: Workers and Technology in the American Auto Industry, 1900-2000" http://www.autolife.umd.umich.edu/Labor/L_Overview/L_Overview8.htm

24. "Thirty Years of Americas Drug War" http://www.pbs.org/wgbh/pages/frontline/shows/drugs/cron

25. 21 U.S.C. § 848: US Code - Section 848: Continuing criminal enterprise http://codes.lp.findlaw.com/uscode/21/13/I/D/848#sthash.N6ZMs1H9.dpuf (2015)

26. "Thirty Years of Americas Drug War" http://www.pbs.org/wgbh/pages/frontline/shows/drugs/cron

27. "Martha Wright Griffiths" http://history.house.gov/People/Listing/G/GRIFFITHS,-Martha-Wright-(G000471)

28. "Shirley Chisholm Biography U.S. Representative (1924–005)" http://www.biography.com/people/shirley-chisholm-9247015#early-life-and-career

29. Grim, Ryan. "Key Figures in CIA-Crack Cocaine Scandal Begin to Come Forward" October 10, 2014. http://www.huffingtonpost.com/2014/10/10/gary-webb-dark-alliance_n_5961748.html and "How John Kerry

Exposed the Iran-Contra Scandal and Showed the Cracks in the War on Drugs" March 13, 2013. http://www.huffingtonpost.com/rick-ross/how-john-kerry-exposed-th_b_2469665.html

30. Grim, Ryan. "Ron Paul Had Accurate Conspiracy Theory: CIA Was Tied to Drug Traffickers" December 12, 2011. http://www.huffingtonpost.com/2011/12/30/ron-paul-conspiracy-theory-cia-drug-traffickers_n_1176103.html

31. The Atlanta Police Department. https://www.joinatlantapd.org/salaryandbenefits.htm (2015)

32. Aamodt, M. G and Stalnaker, N.A. "Police Officer Suicide: Frequency and officer profiles" (June 2006) http://www.policeone.com/health-fitness/articles/137133-Police-Officer-Suicide-Frequency-and-officer-profiles

33. Id http://www.pbs.org/wgbh/pages/frontline/shows/drugs/cron/

34. "32 Individuals Charged in the Largest Drug Trafficking and Money Laundering Case in the Eastern District of Michigan" http://www.dea.gov/pubs/states/newsrel/detroit072005.html

35. Id. http://www.huffingtonpost.com/2011/12/30/ron-paul-conspiracy-theory-cia-drug-traffickers_n_1176103.html

36. id

37. "Department of Justice Statement of Interest Supports Meaningful Right to Counsel in Juvenile Prosecutions" March 2015. http://www.justice.gov/opa/pr/department-justice-

statement-interest-supports-meaningful-right-counsel-juvenile-prosecutions

38. *United States v. Bass*, 404 U.S. 336, 348 (1971)
39. *United States v. Oakland Cannabis Buyer's Cooperative*, 532 U.S. 483, 490 (2001).
40. *Weyhrauch v. United States* 561 US _ (2010) at 71 and *Morales* 527 U.S. at 72 (quotation omitted). https://supreme.justia.com/cases/federal/us/561/08-1394/opinion.html
41. *Skilling v. United States*, 130 S.Ct. 2896 (2010) and *Gonzales v. Carhart*, 550 U.S. 124, 132, 147, 148-49, 149 (2007) (quotation marks and citation partially omitted).
42. "Injury Prevention & Control: Prescription Drug Overdose" http://www.cdc.gov/drugoverdose (2015)
43. "Shirley Chisholm quotes" http://thinkexist.com/quotes/shirley_chisholm (2015)

About The Author

Sherri Jefferson is an author, independent book publisher, attorney, advocate, and lecturer. She is also the founder of the Family Law Center, African American Juvenile Justice Project, Jefferson Publishing, and the Law Mobile. Through #FemaleNOTFeemale, she advocates against child sexual exploitation and sex slavery, and the collateral consequences associated with criminalizing the acts of the victims of human trafficking and prostitution.

www.SherriJefferson.com

www.ingramcontent.com/pod-product-compliance
Lightning Source LLC
Chambersburg PA
CBHW070935130626
46555CB00001B/436